ANGEL

He said, 'Della's been on to me, she complains you don't answer her bell.'

'I was in the garden.'

'That's fine, just tell her when you go out, will you?'

'Okay.'

I don't think that's an unreasonable request. You're there to keep her happy, remember.' A touch of steel in the voice. 'I hope you've everything you want; if not, ask Della, or Mrs Drue, she'll be in again on Monday.'

'Okay.'

'By the way – I might as well tell you now – I'll be down on Friday for the weekend. I'm bringing a friend with me, and two couples will join us on Friday night, you might think up a reasonable dinner – that'll be five extra, Della won't join us.'

'What sort of dinner?' asked Jess, startled.

'*I* don't care. Anything you can do well. Up to you.'

'Seven people altogether.'

'Including you, yes.'

'I wasn't including me, I mean you and Mrs Derby and five guests.'

The slightest pause.

'There is no Mrs Derby.'

How did he expect her to know that? He waited for her to speak but she had nothing to say. He rang off.

To my dear son, with love

Josephine Poole

ANGEL

RED FOX

A Red Fox Book
Published by Arrow Books Limited
20 Vauxhall Bridge Road, London SW1V 2SA

An imprint of Random Century Group

London Melbourne Sydney Auckland
Johannesburg and agencies throughout the world

First published by Hutchinson Children's Books Ltd 1989
Red Fox edition 1991

Set in Sabon
by JH Graphics Ltd, Reading

Made and printed in Great Britain by
Courier International, Tiptree, Essex

ISBN 0 09 973400 1

Angel: Divine messenger . . . lovely or innocent being . . . minister of loving offices . . .

The Concise Oxford Dictionary

One

The hotel lounge was sumptuous, but somehow drab, particularly on a summer day. The sun shone through the net drapes between the tasselled curtains, and lit golden patterns on the carpets and furniture, but the man-made fabrics were designed to resist stains of all sorts, and they flattened the glow. There were paintings of flowers on the walls, but only a few real ones, laid out on the table at the far end of the room. They smelt fresh, whereas the room on the whole had a certain fustiness, as if the invisible stains of that season still hung around in the air.

A waiter was arranging the flowers, mixing real and artificial together in an elegant display that was reflected by the huge mirror behind the table. It was ten o'clock in the morning, and the people who had had breakfast had mostly gone out, while those meeting for coffee had not appeared yet. He expected the lounge to be deserted, and when a blonde girl entered, closely followed by a man, he looked up at once to study them in the mirror. She was very young, tall and well-built. He easily interpreted the flat shoes and light, full-length coat she was wearing – she had not yet come to terms with her height and her figure. He knew the dark-haired man behind her, who often used the hotel, and was called Michael Derby. It seemed almost morally wrong to the waiter, to be able to afford clothes, including shirts and shoes, made to measure at this age – he was perhaps thirty, no more. The two sat down at a corner table, Michael placing the girl so that she faced the light. She was carrying a paper parasol painted with flowers and butterflies, and now made surreptitious efforts to close it, only the catch had jammed. The waiter put down the pink silk carnation he was holding and crossed the room to ask if they wanted coffee.

Michael looked at his companion. 'Do you?'

'Oh – thanks.' She was pink with embarrassment. The waiter, mumuring 'Excuse me,' took the parasol and shut it with a click. He had a close view of her white neck, and bobbed blonde hair which was so thick that it stood out on both sides of her head. She glanced at him thankfully; it was easy to see how nervous she was. He left the room to pass on the order for coffee, and then returned to his flower. The couple intrigued him. She was totally unlike the smart girls he had seen before with Michael Derby.

'Did you have far to come?'

'Oh no – about an hour. You have to change twice. The trains aren't all that frequent.'

'It sounds a long way. I've never been to — where is it?' He opened his pocket book and took out a folded sheet of green paper, which she recognized as her letter. 'Crouch End,' he repeated, as if it was the jungle.

There was a warm silence. The waiter was taking his time with the flowers. Michael was looking at the girl. Her name was Jessica Milton, she lived in Crouch End and she had answered his advertisement. It was not kind to stare at her, but kindness was not a quality people expected in him, and it amused him to see how easily she blushed. Otherwise she was magnolia pale, but he liked the animation in her face. Her blue-grey eyes, when briefly they met his, had darker, sparkling motes in them, as if they reflected lively thoughts, and when she smiled two little vertical lines appeared at each corner of her wide, full-lipped mouth — more interesting than dimples, they made her look altogether older, witty, experienced. Her eyebrows and eyelashes were dark brown, and contrasted strongly with her wiry blonde hair, a blonde that was certainly natural – indeed she wore no make-up at all all. He had already noticed that the dark brows gave force to her frown. Her hands and feet were quite large, her fingers long and bony. She had capable hands, he thought.

'How old are you?' he asked abruptly.

'I've left school,' she answered, too quickly. Evidently she was prepared for that question. 'People are always telling me I look younger than I am.'

'You've told your parents – your family know you're here?'

'Of course!'

A boy in a white jacket brought coffee and biscuits on a tray. Michael poured out as a matter of course, and passed her the biscuits, but she refused, although she was hungry; she couldn't have borne to eat in front of him, dropping crumbs down her front. The coffee was very hot, and tasted as though they hadn't washed out the pot properly. He didn't seem to mind, though she would have judged him one of the complaining sort. He was looking at her letter again while he drank.

'White Posts – that's the name of your house, is it?' He looked her in the eyes as he spoke. His were light brown, very clear and sharp.

'Yes.'

'Just White Posts, Crouch End – not much of an address!'

'It's a pub,' she was forced to admit. She could feel herself blushing again. 'My father's the landlord. We do meals,' she added hopefully, in case that made it sound more elegant.

'You say you know how to cook?'

'I always do the starters and cheescake. Mum does the middle bit, like the game pie or the banger toad – I mean sausage in batter – but if they want Italian I often do it.'

'Anyway you can follow a recipe. Most of the time you'd be cooking for two, but occasionally I'm home for a weekend with guests, or I might want to give a dinner party. I imagine with your training, numbers don't frighten you.'

Jess was beginning, 'We can seat twenty__' but he interrupted her.

'I'm away a lot, so usually there's only Della, my mother-in-law, to worry about. She's not very strong, and needs somebody to run the house, that's to say she wants to do it all herself, but she isn't well enough to manage on her own I'll be frank, she's not that easy to get on with. You could call her a bit of a perfectionist. You need patience, and a sense of humour.'

He thought that Jess had both. He paused, but when she said nothing, went on, 'You'd have your own flat, of course, bathroom, TV and so on. Do you drive?'

'No, I'm__' Jess was beginning, and hastily changed it to, 'I haven't got around to it yet.'

'It doesn't matter, except that the house is rather isolated, or some people might think so. The nearest town is about eight miles away, but there's a village with shops within walking distance. What other interests do you have, apart from cooking?'

'I don't know. I like music.' It sounded inadequate. 'I like walking anyway, I like the country.'

'That's all right then. More coffee?'

'No, thanks.'

He glanced at his watch, and put away her letter. He was aware that the waiter had been watching them in the mirror, although he was too far away to hear what they said. Now he caught his eye in the glass. The man, confused, turned his whole attention to the flower arrangement, and presently left the room.

'What else do you want to know? Della's got a son, Christian, my brother-in-law. He's off to college in September but he may be around some of the time. In terms of physical labour there isn't much, the house is full of mod cons and does everything itself except dust and polish, and a woman comes up from the village to do that. It's really a question of providing edible meals, and keeping Della happy. Oh – wages, of course__' and here he mentioned a sum that seemed wonderfully large to Jess. 'What do you think? I'm afraid I can't take ditherers – if it isn't yes, it's no.'

'You mean, you aren't seeing anyone else?'

'Why should I?'

'Oh. Yes, please.'

This was obviously the answer he expected. He said, 'I've got your number on your letter. I'll ring tonight and talk to your Mum, in case she thinks you're being abducted. You said you could start at once. There's a bus straight through, and I'll arrange for you to be met the other end, but I'll confirm all that on the phone.

They got up, and she followed him out of the

lounge, observing him as she hadn't dared to do face to face. His hair was black and curly, and cut short, but not shaved at the back, so that little dark curls lay against his brown neck, a tan he must have got abroad, because until today it had been a miserable summer. His collar was spotlessly white, his city suit dark and trim. She couldn't tell that it had been made for him, but she saw how well he looked in it, even from behind. His manner was both casual and alert; he moved like an athlete. This was her first interview, and she hadn't expected to get the job. He was to be her employer, and she was relieved that he had said he would be away most of the time. She was not entirely confident of her ability to run the kind of household he had described, and she guessed that he was not one to suffer fools gladly.

They went through the revolving doors, which hushed them out into the dazzling street. He walked with her without speaking, as far as the flower barrow, where he bought all the freesias they had and gave them to her, presenting them without a smile, or any softening of his sharp look; then he said, 'I'll be in touch,' and turning, hailed a cab which seemed to appear magically at his convenience, got in and was driven away. Jess was left balancing her parasol and the flowers, staring after him.

Two

The first hot day this summer people told each other, and city tempo visibly slackened. Out came the sun-tops, the boxer shorts, the mini and ra-ra skirts, new and old fashions – anything went on a day like this. Noise blared out of open windows; smells were sharper, peppery in the nose. Dirt looked dirtier. People swilled drinks and kippered themselves in parks, on the grass that was still damp to lie on; and in the whole of north London, only one girl was wearing a coat. That was Jess, coming down the long hill from the station, holding the sunshade upside down in front of her like a tray.

Her younger sister Josie had pushed out the moustached plywood figure, lifesize in white overalls and chef's hat more like a bowler, which advertised HOME COOKING in front of the White Posts. Now she waited, shading her eyes against the sun with one hand whose fingernails were painted different colours, a bright red lipstick on her babyish mouth which easily looked discontented. Jess steadily approached the billowing coat, like a ship in full sail, and then Josie saw the reason for the parasol tray.

'Flowers? Where from?'

'He gave them to me.'

'This Mr Derby? Why?'

Jess looked down, surprised, at the freesias. 'I don't know. I thought it was nice.'

Josie's busy mind was considering possibilities. 'What's he like?'

'Okay.'

Okay! What could you tell from that? 'Well, but have you got it? Did he give you the job?'

'Yes.'

'Are you taking it? Is it good money?'

'Yes and yes.'

A shriek from indoors. They moved at once to the pub entrance, through the beer smell hanging like a curtain. It suddenly struck Josie that Jess was about to escape from her dogsbody position in the family, and she turned hot with the injustice of it, and crossly remarked, 'I don't know what Mum will say about him buying you *flowers*,' as if they were underwear.

'She won't mind.' Jess spoke with the calm assurance that often kept the household peace.

'You might lay up for me. I've been on the go all morning.' Josie had been in bed when Jess left the house. 'They want it in the garden. It's too hot. I wish I was in Majorca. Eight of them, Mum said to join tables. Tell her I've gone for the mayonnaise.'

That meant she would meet her friends on the corner; Jess had passed them, hanging around for Josie, but for once she didn't care. Her feet were light on the stairs and she was smiling as she went into the little bedroom she had always shared with her sister. She put her coat and parasol of flowers on the bed, and looked round, noticing as if she was a stranger the cheap furniture, the cracked lino on the floor, the ceiling so low that for years she had had to duck to look out of the window. It would be marvellous –

marvellous to leave home! It was unbelievable luck to have her feet already on the threshold!

She could hear her mother slamming about in the kitchen, and went straight out into the garden to arrange tables. They were a junky lot but two more or less matched, and she pulled them together, with benches to seat eight. Conscious all the time of her mother's eyes through the window, she expected a tap on the glass. But she was full of happiness, and in order to get it under control, make her face acceptable to the parent she was leaving tomorrow – tomorrow! – she lingered by the rickety fence, picking up the litter that always blew along it.

The garden was about a third the size of a tennis court, mostly grass kept short by the feet of the customers. Two concrete posts supported a clematis and a climbing rose, which were supposed to screen the little yard where the dustbins stood, and the old rabbit hutch. There were red and white striped garden umbrellas, printed with the name of a brewery, though it was Doc's ambition to have his own pub, that was what his wife and daughters were working for. Abandoned on the grass was a little trolley of wooden bricks that had belonged, like the rabbit, first to Jess, then to Josie; now visiting children sometimes played with it, and sometimes they gave the rabbit, sunbathing in his box, scraps of unwanted salad, or a dandelion discovered in the grit along the fence.

The kitchen window snapped open. 'I could do with some help in here!'

Jess dropped the litter in the bin and went indoors. She began loading a tray with salts and peppers, little bottles of vinegar, sets of knives and forks wrapped in paper napkins.

'You may as well lay for more than just eight,' said Mrs Milton, without turning round. 'There'll be a crowd this weather. Where's Josie?'

'Gone for the mayonnaise.'

'Don't we know what that means.' She sniffed. 'How did you get on, anyway?'

'I got the job.'

'I can see that, but exactly what sort of work is it? As I remember the ad was rather vague on that point.'

'Housekeeping. For a lady. She's not well, it's running the house for her.'

Exit Jess with tray to the garden. Her mother thought it over while she put the clean lettuce in the plastic baskets, sliced tomatoes. Her hands worked automatically, nervously efficient. All the time she was aware of her daughter taking her time over the tables.

'I thought it was a man you saw,' she said, when Jess came back at last with the empty tray.

'It's for his mother-in-law.'

'Whereabouts is it? I'm not having you going miles away from home.'

'I don't know.'

'But he must have said – this Mr Derby. He must have told you.'

'I should have asked. I forgot.'

'Well, and did you meet this sick woman?'

'Only him, but he was nice.'

'He would be, wouldn't he. When does he want you to start?'

'He's ringing tonight.'

'I see, and I'll speak to him, please.'

'That's why he's ringing,' said Jess with a flash of anger.

'I don't know why you've got this bee in your bonnet about going away on a job when there's plenty to do here, heaven knows. I suppose Rachel's off on all sorts.' Rachel was Jess's friend. 'All sorts' was Judy Milton's phrase for dubious activities. 'If it's genuine housekeeping I'd have thought he'd have wanted an older girl. Does he know your age?'

'He wasn't worried.'

'I don't mind telling you I don't like the sound of it. These days you've got to be so careful. I can see you've set your heart on it, but in the end it's not for you to decide. If your father and I think it's unsuitable, that's it, my girl, you can't go.'

'I'm sixteen!'

'What difference does that make? You're naive – gullible. Josie knows more about life than you do!'

Jess's throat swelled with hot rebellious words. She had never argued with her mother, or let herself take much notice of these opinions often expressed, and hurtful just the same. But now she suddenly said, 'You only say that to hold me back. It's not true. I'd be a fool to act like Josie.' Her hands trembled as she stacked the tray with baskets of food.

Her mother was taken aback. She was about to return a sharp answer, when she heard the first customers coming in from the pavement. She pulled off her apron and hurried through to the bar, leaving Jess to carry the tray into the garden, so full of a sense of injustice that she wanted to cry. It was no use appealing to her father, who invariably kept out of reach when there was a family drama. He was a big, blond, easy-going man; Jess had inherited his physique, and he loved her for it, but not enough to defy his wife.

That day seemed longer than other days. It was as if the city, now it had a taste of summer, held on to it beyond the prescribed sunset hour. People lingered in the gardens, the streets; as the noise of traffic diminished, the voices and pop music took over. On the gritty lawn behind the White Posts, the families took a long time finishing their drinks. The Miltons were on their feet for hours; the drawer of the till was stiff with money. And all the time Jess had an ear cocked for the phone, but it was Josie who got to it first, scuttering down the dark passage and snatching up the receiver just as her sister made a dive for it. 'Whayte Posts,' she said, in what she called her sophisticated voice.

'It's mine,' Jess hissed. Her eyes gleamed like a cat's. But Josie staring at her shook her head, covered the mouthpiece and said, 'It's not, it's Mum. *Mum*!' she shrieked. They paused, glaring at each other, breathing hard, listening to the gabble from the bar. 'Wan moment,' said Josie into the phone. 'I'll just give her another call. *Mum*!' she shrieked again, forgetting this time to shield the mouthpiece, as Judy Milton appeared from the kitchen, wiping her hands on her apron.

'We're busy tonight, you'll have to speak up,' she said curtly. Jess felt sick. She went to the kitchen and sat down at the table, fixing her eyes blankly on the garden which was getting dark at last. A girl was laughing out there, but Jess didn't hear her. He was standing at the telephone, surrounded by her impression of the hotel which was vague but lush. His spotlessly white shirt was open at the throat, his brown hand masterful on the receiver. Josie had just deafened him, her mother was being rude; but Jess dreamed, automatically eating prawns out of a basket which happened to be in front of her. She was roused by her mother.

'*What the goodness* are you doing? Somebody's paid for that!' She snatched the basket away, fluffed up the lettuce with agitated fingers and threw on more prawns. 'Here, take this through – number three,' and she turned quickly to the sink, without giving anything away.

Jess met Josie in the passage and thrust the prawns at her. 'Number three,' she snapped, and returned to the kitchen. Her mother was loading the dishwasher. Jess handed glasses, eyeing her silently, and felt a sudden flutter of excitement. Mum was undoubtedly impressed. All the same, she broached the subject in an accusing tone.

'You didn't tell me he was with Illuminations.'

'He never said.'

'Not the Group,' breathed Josie, coming in at that moment.

'Illuminations *Inc*, the oil people. Well he must be a very rich man. He seems to want you, Jess. I hope you're listening, Josie. Your sister always worked harder than you do, and now she's had a lucky break. It sounds a nice place I'm glad to say, since you're so set on it, and he made a point of asking us over to visit you whenever we like, not that we'll have the time, but it was thoughtful of him.'

'I want to go,' whined Josie. 'It's my summer holidays.'

'You'll have plenty to do here without Jess. She was my right hand at your age.'

Doc Milton put his head round the door. Even his daughters called him Doc, from an old joke nobody now remembered. 'Two ham and pickle, one cheese without,' he said. 'What's this, a sit-down?'

'Jess has just landed herself a job. Living in, on higher wages than I've ever earned. Or ever been able to pay, for that matter.'

'Maybe so but we can't spare her.'

'Rubbish! Any kid off the Work Experience could do what Jess does here. It's time she got out of the pub. She's made the effort, and I shan't stand in her way.' Judy was buttering bread for the sandwiches. Jess kept her eyes on the cheese she was slicing. Her mother's tone was as sharp as ever, but her words were revealing, and Jess had a sudden glimpse of what she endured with Doc, who was always going places but never arrived.

He went back to the bar, expressing defeat even from the back, like an actor – head thrust forward a little, shoulders drooping, the slightest shuffle in the walk. So that people would ask, 'What's up Doc? Anything wrong?' and when Jess followed him a minute later with the plates of sandwiches, she caught the sympathetic platitudes, 'They can't wait to leave home . . . Don't stay young long these days . . .' He turned to her and said, 'Give your old Dad a kiss then,' and she put up her face so that he could kiss her cheek. But she couldn't get used to the beard which was of recent growth. It was stronger in texture and colour than his skimpy hair had ever been, and had a moist feeling.

Her arrangements were discussed sporadically, as work permitted. Mr Derby wanted her to start tomorrow. 'Short notice!' grumbled Doc. 'He knows his own mind, that's what I like about him. Straightforward,' said Judy. 'I hope she's got the money for the fare. I'm sure I haven't. I wasn't expecting this.' 'She can borrow from the till. You talk as if we're paupers. One single fare, on the coach.' 'What's all the rush, I'd like to know? Funny way to do business if you ask me,' he groused. 'I've got nothing against it. If she's going, she might as well go. Besides, there's an invalid at the house, you can't argue where health's concerned.' 'I hope it isn't catching, that's all.'

Jess was dismissed to pack. She took over all the articles she shared with Josie – The Dressing Gown, The Hair Conditioner, The Handmirror, and so on, stuffing as much as she could into The Suitcase, and then filling several plastic bags. The coach for Palmers Cross left Victoria at lunchtime tomorrow, and she would be met at the bus stop. There wasn't even time to ring Rachel and tell her the news, but in fact she didn't want to share it. Rachel had a way of breaking things down; she would insist on a full description of Michael Derby and she wouldn't understand why Jess hadn't found out more about his work and his wife and the house and his in-laws. So Jess was glad to forgo this conversation, though it was Rachel who had spotted the advertisement in one of the weekly papers in her mother's hairdressing salon, which gave her a right to know.

Josie slammed into bed very late, and lay snuffling into her pillow, needing to make friends again before she went to sleep. But Jess stayed awake long after that. The darkness, which hid so much, opened her senses more than was possible during daytime with its crowding impressions. By night she could hear the ticking of the downstairs clock; the creak of her parents' bed and words between them spoken in low voices. She could tell when Josie slipped from the threshold of sleep, into its deep interior. Still she lay with a quickly beating heart, and tried to lull herself by picking out faces in the uneven glass of the window pane, where it gleamed in the yellow shine of a street lamp. But *his* face eluded her, though his freesias were like a magic spell in their vase between the beds, drowning, for the first time in her life the smell of beer.

Three

The Bell House stood on a little hill, a mile or so from Palmers Cross. It was built of red brick, in the style of an old-fashioned dolls' house – double-fronted, with the front door and four downstairs windows corresponding exactly to five above. It had a beautiful garden. Several huge oak trees had been trapped there, as well as a section of river which had been widened to make a swimming pool before it escaped across the fields. Altogether the place looked a 'handsome property', or even 'small country estate', but in fact the agent had had it on his books for several months before Sylvie Derby fell in love with it. It was not grand enough, or it was too grand for commerical purposes; it needed a private owner with plenty of money.

There was nothing Sylvie liked better than spending Michael's money. So he bought the Bell House, partly to please her, partly because it was big enough to include her family with the minimum of inconvenience to himself. He put in a tennis court, and converted the top floor into a studio where she could paint if she felt like it, with a baby grand for her musical moments. As time passed, his work occupied him more and more, and he travelled a good deal, alone, because she hated flying. Luckily she had her mother to keep her company, as well as her brother

Christian during holidays from his expensive school (Michael paid the fees). This isolated domesticity suited him because it never impinged on his professional activities, but if he was independent, so was she, and he had to put up with that. Still, for a young couple who had married for worldly reasons – he for her beauty, she for his cash – it should have been an ideal arrangement.

That was six years ago. Things had changed since that gilt-edged beginning; now Michael did not come home very often to the Bell House.

Della's room was on the first floor, with a bird's-eye view over the front garden and drive. Michael had telephoned her yesterday to tell her that Jess was coming, and now she was on the alert in her armchair near the window her workbox on a little table beside her. She was making him a shirt of cream silk; her needle flew, picking up tiny stitches. The strain of sewing without spectacles showed in her face, particularly in her eyes which were brown and slightly protuberant. Her straight, shoulder-length dark hair, barely streaked with silver, was held back with a plain black band. Most women of her age wouldn't have dared to wear it like that, but it suited her. She was slender, and perfectly groomed in a comfortable old tailor-made skirt and cashmere jumper. Her stockings never had a ladder, her shoes were always polished. She only wore make-up to enhance her naturally beautiful features, the lightest touch of rouge on her high cheek bones, a suspicion of browny-pink colour on her full lips. She never lounged, or slouched, though more and more often now she had to pause on her way upstairs, with a fluttering sensation, the edge of pain in her thin chest.

The girl before Jess had stayed a fortnight.

The weather was warm, but cloudy. So far it had been a dismal summer, and Della fancied that the leaves on the oaks had a yellowish tinge already, in August. The border was only colourful from a distance. Roses grew directly below her window, and their scent should have drifted into the room. But the blooms had lost their proper, compact brightness; they were floppy, dishevelled, their fragrance wasted.

The rhythm of her needle was interrupted, only for a stitch, by the sound of feet on the stairs. Life at the Bell House would have stopped without Mrs Drue, who was laundress, cleaner and polisher, and runner of errands in her swift scarlet Mini. If she had no indoor tasks, she turned gardener, and now as she knocked and entered one could see she had the shape for it, being bulky below the waist, in brown crimplene trousers and sensible laced shoes. From such a base she could easily duck head and shoulders among the plants.

Della extracted the weekly wage envelope from her workbox.

'I'll be off now, Mrs Fry – unless you want me to stay on for the new girl.'

'That's not necessary, thank you,' said Della, with a pleasant smile. She passed the envelope, and returned to her sewing. She did not want conversation, and knew how to discourage it. Mrs Drue had once hinted that she had seen a ghost in Sylvie's bedroom. Della loathed that kind of gossip.

Mrs Drue said provocatively, 'I hope *this* young lady will be a success.'

'I hope so.' Della kept her eyes on the seam.

'Till next week, then, Mrs Fry.'

'Thank you. Have a good weekend.'

'And you.'

The door closed. Presently the helper bowled away. The Bell House was now empty but for Della, its parquet shining in a vacuum, its mod cons quiescent, only its clocks, little and big, marking the pulse of time.

Della was panicky about being alone in the house. She glanced at her watch. The London coach would call at Palmers Cross in about twenty minutes, and she had booked the taxi to meet it. The way to face time, half an hour, or days or weeks, was to divide it into manageable sections. Ten minutes' sewing. Five minutes to wash, comb her hair, check her complexion; ten more to get herself downstairs, look into the kitchen and the big rooms, the girl's flat. So she was standing in the doorway, smiling and unrushed, as the taxi scrunched up the drive. No one would have known that she was silly about first meetings, that her left hand was clutching the emergency pills in her skirt pocket. Her welcoming expression did not falter. But, oh dear, what was Michael thinking of? Bare legs – *Sandals* – one of those full skirts made of cheap Indian cotton in a pastel blue that showed every mark of the journey – a big, blonde girl – dear God, what age could she be? She looked like a school child!

Jess looked shyly at Della. Most girls would have been struck by her faultless appearance, but Jess often missed what was obvious to others, and she didn't notice it. She saw her as frail, somewhat sharp – school-mistressy she would have said, although the teachers at her school had none of them looked like that. She turned to grapple with her luggage, and dropped a plastic bag which leaked a pair of tights onto the drive. 'Let him see to your things my dear, I expect you're tired after your journey. No, no you *don't* need to pay – that's already settled.' Della stood aside for Jess to enter, followed by the taxi driver with his head down, managing the suitcase and the carriers. He dumped them in the hall and went away.

The clouds had cleared while Della was waiting for the taxi, pushing away from a wide and wider blue, and now the hall was suddenly full of sunlight which warmed the arrangement of scarlet flowers in the corner, the oriental rugs on the fudge-coloured parquet. But above all it shone in Jess's hair, which was inclined to stand out, as if it was somehow more lively than most people's, and made it positively electrical, a mass of individually glittering wires. She looked about with her diffident yet humorous gaze, from the ivory walls to the jade green stair carpet to the dull but costly pictures with their jade mounts and ivory frames. Then she gathered her luggage, and followed Della down the hall to a little passage with a door at the end.

'This is your flat. It's quite self-contained, and no one will disturb you. You should find everything you need. Have you been away from home before?'

'Yes.' Rache had been to Caen with the school, she could use that. But Della didn't ask for details. Jess looked past her into the bedroom. The towels, chair seats, curtains, counterpane all matched, flowers on a green background that went with the carpet. She put her suitcase on the bed, then lifted it off at once in case it marked the cover. She stood there awkwardly, clutching her things.

'I'll leave you to sort yourself out. I expect you'd like

a cup of tea; I'll put the kettle on. Join me in the kitchen when you're ready.'

The door closed softly. Jess stared round. She wanted to run away, she wanted to laugh. She felt hysterical. French window on to walled courtyard with white-painted outbuildings and bed of begonias! En suite bathroom with fitted carpet, shower, toilet – even a bidet! Alcove with armchair and colour telly! She changed her skirt for a clean one, and bent to the three-piece mirror to brush her hair, which seemed to want to stand on end with astonishment. The whole place was straight out of Rache's Mum's mags! She couldn't believe people's cooks lived like this; they would expect a French menu, or worse, some horribly complicated diet. It was a sobering thought. The very word 'starter' seemed suddenly unsuitable. Mrs Fry had probably never tasted Thousand Island sauce.

She opened the door into the house, and Della who had been listening for it, called, 'This way!' Jess nearly lost her balance on the parquet, and appeared in the kitchen less calmly than she would have liked. Della was sitting at the table, very upright on a brightly coloured stool. Tea was in cups with saucers, the biscuits were on a plate. Jess seemed to hear her mother's voice, 'You'll have to drop your slovenly habits, my girl!'

'We try to keep up to date with improvements,' said Della, noticing the glazed eyes of her companion wandering around the room. 'Do you use a microwave?'

'Not really.' Doc was keen, but Mum wouldn't have it. Black mark number one.

'I don't care for it myself, but you'll be glad of it

when Michael brings down a party from London, for instance when the shooting starts.'

Shooting! Jess was speechless. She gulped her tea. Della drank in sips, observing her over the rim of her cup.

'What do you think of this tea?'

'It's very nice.'

'It's a jasmine. I have it specially blended. I'm glad you like it. Coarse teas are so bad for the digestion.'

They sat in silence for several minutes. Some of the gadgets shining in that kitchen were total strangers to Jess. If she broke anything, it would cost a lot.

'Do you always wear a skirt?' Della asked unexpectedly.

'I don't like myself in trousers.'

'How sensible! There's nothing more attractive than a full skirt, and pretty feet in nice, flat, summery shoes.' They both looked at Jess's feet which were too big for prettiness. 'The last girl wore elastic jeans all the time with very high heels. More tea?'

'No, I won't, thanks.'

'Would you like to see round the house, and then I can explain about locking up at the same time. No, *don't* stack the china in the sink, *please* – it's sure to get chipped! We have a machine that does all the washing-up, far more thoroughly and kindly than you or I could do it,' and she indicated a stainless steel monster with a complicated dial screwed into its forehead.

They left the kitchen and crossed the hall to the drawing-room. Here the colour scheme was reversed, the curtains and upholstery being ivory with a gold motif, the walls jade green. There was only one picture which hung over the marble fireplace at the end of the room. It was an oil painting of a girl, a very beautiful girl in a black frock. Her curly golden hair was cut short like a boy's, her brown eyes stared at them with an impatient, challenging expression. She looked clever, wilful, dynamic; the painting was technically so excellent that one assumed it was an exact likeness.

'Is that Mrs Derby – your daughter?'

'Yes, that's Sylvie.' There was nothing in Della's tone to encourage questions. She began explaining how the shutters were to be closed and barred every night. 'It's most important. Michael collects antiques, as you've probably noticed. Several pieces in here are Chippendale.'

'I thought they were mahogany,' said Jess, innocently.

Della looked oddly at her. They went into the next room with its oval dinning table and leather seated chairs. On the sideboard the cruets, coasters and so on were polished almost to blindness by the attentive Mrs Drue, whose hand had placed one perfect rose in a cut glass dish dead centre. The thought of making food for such a table was terrifying, and Jess was glad when they shut the door, and went slowly upstairs. They had to wait a minute on the landing for Della to get her breath. Her hand on the banister was surprisingly hard-worked; there had been a time when she stripped wallpaper and lined ceilings, before she reached the top of the interior decorating business. The most expensive cream couldn't ladyfy her hands.

'This is me,' she said, clearing her throat in a nervous way she had, and leading the way into her bedroom. 'If I have a bad day, and feel I can't tackle the stairs, I can be comfortable up here with all my things round me. I'm glad to say I have plenty to occupy my mind. I may be a semi-invalid, but I hope I still take an interest in what goes on in the world.' She moved to the window. 'I can enjoy the garden from here, almost as much as if I was sitting outside. That's the road to the village. I can keep an eye on all the comings and goings.'

Jess stood beside her, looking out at the steep view of the garden now glowing in evening sunshine, and the sloping fields and the lane beyond.

'Did Michael mention my son to you?' Della broke the silence.

'Yes he did.'

'He's not here at present. I never know what his movements are. He comes and goes.'

Jess said nothing. A blackbird flew into the hedge, and sang a few notes, as sweet and clear as if its beak was full of honey. Della said, 'This is the first summer evening we've had.'

'It was hot yesterday, in London.'

'Then you've brought it with you.' She turned to her chair, and sat down. 'I shan't bother you much in the morning. I have my own teamaker, my special bran biscuits, and that's all I take until lunchtime, when I like a little poached fish with spinach and an egg sauce, or perhaps a soufflé – something very light and easy, anyhow. Of course it's different when Michael's down – did he mention how soon he might be coming?'

'No.'

'He's very good, he never descends without warning. I like to have the house ready for him – fresh flowers in the vases, clean sheets on all the beds, and so on. But you can leave that side of it to Mrs Drue, she's been with us years and knows exactly how we do things. Now you must let me rest, I'm getting breathless. I'll ring this bell when I need you.' she pressed a buzzer, which made Jess jump. 'You're free to unpack now, and then I daresay you'll want to watch TV. I hardly look at it, but I expect you like it. I don't want to be demanding on your first evening, two ham sandwiches will be plenty for my supper, if you could bring them punctually at eight; and then I take a mug of Horlicks and an oatmeal biscuit at nine. I like everything locked up by nine-thirty, and if you could look in to say goodnight when you've done that.'

'Okay,' said Jess, her brain reeling. 'Can I get you anything now?'

'No thank you, my dear. A little peace and quiet is all I need.'

Jess went out and closed the door. She was on the stairs when the buzzer grabbed her.

'I forgot to tell you to get your own supper. There's a good selection of food in the fridge. Take what you like.'

'Okay. Thanks.'

This time she got downstairs before the buzzer bit.

'Could you shut the window, do you think? Thanks so much. The catch is rather stiff.'

It didn't take Jess long to arrange her things in the drawers and fitted cupboards. Then she opened the French window, and stepped into the courtyard. There was a white-painted door which must lead to the garden. It was locked but the key was on her side; she turned it, and went through.

Michael had had this part of the garden levelled for

the tennis court. A path of mown grass led past it, to the slope where the oaks still grew. On the left, the softly undulating country stretched as far as the eye could see, with black and white cows in the fields, or yellow ripening wheat. Jess wondered if she would ever get used to the quietness of it. Her ears ached, anticipating a traffic jam, a burst of pop music – even the Italian takeaway next door to the White Posts having one of their rows. The path continued away from the house, beyond the reach of Della's scanning eye, and she was glad about that. It wasn't quite seven, so she had plenty of time. Soon she left the orbit of the motor mower for rough tussocky grass between natural thickets of thorn and hazel; and there, unexpectedly, was the river. In fact she'd been listening to it as she walked, without realizing what it could be.

It got in through a culvery under the lane, and now, trapped for a while in the wilderness at the Bell House, continued its steady, shallow progress, so clear that the waterweeds, all trailing one way like green hair, could be seen right down to their roots in the speckled brown gravelly bottom. Further along, three wide stone steps had been constructed, down which the water flowed, shining and unhurried, and below these slowly moving stairs the river bed had been widened to make a bathing pool, which was bounded at the far end by a heavy stone balustrade. The water appeared to hang suspended on the other side of this in several shining streams, which dropped down the hillside to meet in a foaming pool at the bottom, before continuing its leisurely way among the fields.

This part of the garden often flooded, and even now it was soft underfoot. A stone temple, or sort of grandiose bathing shelter, had been built at the same time as the pool. There was a compartment for changing in, and a pavement where people could sit and watch the swimmers, or changing the position of their chairs, admire the view. It was not yet dark, but lights were already pricking out across country. Even on the clearest day, towns and villages were lost in the gently contoured, wooded landscape, but at night they appeared in bright clusters.

There was a deckchair on the pavement, which had been there so long that its stripes had faded to grey. Jess had the impression, from this, or the cracks in the temple, or simply because the shadows were lengthening with evening, that people didn't come here any more. She looked across the water. The opposite bank was thick with rushes and wild iris, and huge leaves like umbrellas. Trees grew above, and almost hidden among them she made out an odd little tower, topped with an arched belfry from which the house must have got its name.

Swimming was the one sport Jess excelled at. She took off her sandals, her skirt and blouse, and gingerly dipped one foot into the water. Oh, but it was cold, cold! All the greyness of grey days seemed accumulated in it. She struck out from the grassy edge, gasping with the shock of it, her white arms flashing with a silvery shine; she swam to the watery steps where the river came in, like a tame jacuzzi, and then she flogged down to the balustrade, making good speed with what current there was behind her. She was warmer now, and turning on to her back, floated with the infinite depth of darkening sky above her. After a little while, magically, one star blinked and glowed, like a chink into a different world.

A church bell struck in the distance, one flat note.

Jess glanced at her watch – and saw to her horror that it was already half-past seven. She swam to the pavement, clambered out and rubbed herself with the chiffon scarf she'd used to tie back her hair. More wet than dry, she pulled on her clothes, pushed her feet into her sandals, and ran all the way back to the house. The buzzer noise greeted her as she entered; Della was sitting with her finger on the button.

She flew upstairs, and knocked on the door. 'Is that you at last, Jessica?' faintly, from the chair.

'Yes.'

'Well, come right in, please. It's exhausting to speak with one's head twisted round.'

Jess crossed the room. She was surprised to see how dark the garden looked from the lamplit interior. Della too looked dark, thin, peevish.

'Where have you been? I buzzed and buzzed. Didn't you hear the bell?'

'I was in the garden.'

'But your hair's all wet! It's not raining, is it?'

'I just washed it. After the journey.' It sounded like a lie. Jess grinned, embarrassed; turned it into a grimace; bit her thumbnail; joined her hands behind her back. She saw that she had upset Della. 'I need some fresh air,' she explained.

'But I wish you'd told me. I don't at all mind being alone, provided I know where you are. And now you're dripping all over the carpet! Go along and dry your hair. It's almost eight o'clock, and irregular meals always give me indigestion, but that can't be helped.'

The evening had begun badly. It got worse.

'Do you always make your sandwiches like this?'

Della asked, raising her eyes from the plate, as Jess was about to leave the room.

'What's wrong with them?'

'Please, don't be aggressive. I don't want to be difficult, but I do like my bread sliced thinly, and the crusts taken off.'

And again, 'I'm sorry to have to say this, Jessica, but it would have been thoughtful of you to trim the ham. I am absolutely unable to eat fat.'

And later still, 'Is this English mustard?'

'I think so.'

'I always eat French.'

So that by the time Jess sat down to her own supper in the kitchen, with the only cookery book she could find spread out in front of her, she began to think that she would earn her wages.

What was a soufflé? How did you poach fish? What was egg sauce? She had looked into the deep freeze and found only vegetables there. The kitchen was full of gadgets but did not include a deep fryer, or even a sandwich maker; toasted cheese, scampi and chips were out. She was worried. Her lips moved as she skimmed through the recipes.

At half-past nine she took Della her Horlicks and biscuit, half an hour late because supper had been late. Yes, she had locked and bolted the front door and the back door; yes, she was quite certain she had closed all the downstairs windows, barred the shutters, and switched on the alarm.

'Very well, then please draw the curtains for me. No, *not* like that—' the head moved irritably against the cushioned back of the chair. 'You'll spoil the hang of the fabric, and no matter how clean your hands are, in time the edges will get grubby. Pull the cord at the side.' The heavy curtains with their dull pink and grey pattern of smudged magnolias swung across. 'That's right. Now fill my teamaker, please, not too full, it's clearly marked inside – no, *not* from the bathroom tap! Take it down to the kitchen, that's the only drinkable water in the house, but be sure to let it run first, so that it's perfectly cold and fresh.'

Jess did this. She also folded the counterpane, fluffed up the pillows, turned down the bed, extracted the nightdress from its hand-embroidered case and hung it over the towel rail, ran the bath. Meanwhile Della with exquisite care was folding her sewing between layers of tissue paper which she then, with her characteristic little clearing of the throat, slid into a bag. 'I can't sew any more tonight,' she remarked plaintively. 'I try not to complain but at night my arms feel so heavy, it's an effort even to brush my hair as much as I would like.' Jess knew what was coming. 'Could you__ But no, I won't ask you your first evening. I daresay you're tired. You run along now, have a good rest. I expect you're a heavy sleeper – I'll try not to disturb you. I never ring at night unless I really need something.'

'Goodnight then.'

'Goodnight, Jessica.'

She went downstairs to the kitchen, and cleared away her solitary meal. The only bread here was brown, full of seeds and fibres; they always bought white sliced at home. This time yesterday she was eating a chicken leg in her fingers, standing by the dresser because the kitchen table was covered with dirty dishes. Today had been in front of her like a present, wrapped up and full of promise, with the family agog for her to open it? Supposing she called them now and told them about it? Josie would have walked out by this time.

At that moment, aptly, the phone rang. Jess, in a panic not to disturb Della, snatched for the instrument placed between the dresser and the steam extractor. Her stool tottered and crashed.

'Hello?' Mum? Josie, perhaps?

'Broken?' The question was put in an agreeable tone. Michael Derby.

'Oh! No, it's okay. Only the stool. Sorry.'

'That's all right. Were you expecting someone else to ring?'

'No – why?'

'You sounded disappointed. – You're not homesick, are you?'

'Of course not!'

There was a pause. She guessed that he didn't believe her. He said, 'Della's been on to me, she complains you don't answer her bell.'

'I was in the garden.'

'That's fine, just tell her when you go out, will you.'

'Okay.'

'I don't think that's an unreasonable request. You're there to keep her happy, remember.' A touch of steel in the voice. 'I hope you've everything you want; if not, ask Della, or Mrs Drue, she'll be in again on Monday.'

'Okay.'

'By the way – I might as well tell you now – I'll be down on Friday for the weekend. I'm bringing a friend with me, and two couples will join us on Friday night, you might think up a reasonable dinner – that'll be five extra, Della won't join us.'

'What sort of dinner?' asked Jess, startled.

'I don't care. Anything you can do well. Up to you.'

'Seven people altogether.'

'Including you, yes.'

'I wasn't including me, I mean you and Mrs Derby and five guests.'

The slightest pause.

'There is no Mrs Derby.'

How did he expect her to know that? He waited for her to speak but she had nothing to say. He rang off.

Four

That night was completely still, and so clear that the man in the moon seemed to be peering directly down into the garden of the Bell House, with his distorted face that looked as if he had had a stroke. By his light one could have counted the blades of grass, or ripples on the pool. Because soon after midnight there were ripples, even in that stillness, and suddenly a splash by the edge, as a youth pulled himself up out of the water.

He paused to shake the water out of his hair and ears, and then he padded down the path towards the house, across the gibbous shadow cast by the temple, between the bushes which looked more substantial by moonlight. Obviously he knew the garden, for he moved without hesitation, turning to pass tennis court in the direction of the outbuildings and the service flat. When he reached the wall, he didn't try the door, though Jess had in fact forgotten to lock it as she sped through. He leapt, lithe and effortless as a cat, grabbed two of the pointed stones that capped it, and pulled himself up. He poised a moment, balanced on the uneven summit, before he dropped noiselessly into the courtyard and began creeping round it, ready at the least disturbance to melt into the shadows.

Jess had left the French window ajar. The boy raised one hand and switched off the alarm, then he pushed aside the curtain and edged through. There she lay in the bed within his reach, palely asleep on her back, her hair a silvery mass round her unconscious face. He was alert, and could have let go the curtain in an instant, but it wasn't necessary. So he looked, long and long.

Perhaps he got into her dreams, as Cupid or Prince Charming. For he resembled a young god, almost naked, his hair crumpling into curls as the water dried. At any rate, his going disturbed her. He was just disappearing over the wall when the pattern of her curtains glowed as she switched on the light. But she didn't look between them, and the wet footprints round her window soon vanished in the warm air.

Five

Della never gave anyone the sack – she never had to. Those who were not monuments of patience, or, like Mrs Drue, tuned to a supernatural wavelength, left quickly, maddened by her quirks and foibles. But as Jess had never worked away before, she had only home standards to compare with the way things were run at the Bell House. Her own mother was hard enough to please. So although she made faces going up and down stairs, and muttered in the kitchen, on the whole she kept her temper.

The proposed dinner weighed heavily on her mind, and making a mess of Della's lunch on Saturday did nothing for her self-confidence. Della lifted a little with her fork, and looked across at Jess who was waiting, pink and mortified.

'This is a little unexpected,' she said. 'Au gratin means a cheese sauce. How do you usually serve your plaice?'

'*Batter*!' There was a poignant pause. 'There's a tin of shrimp bisque in the larder, Jessica – could you heat that for me? *Don't* let it boil. I'll have that, with some toast – I'm not very hungry. One thing – I'm told it would be bad for me to put on weight. I shan't do that while you're here, shall I?' with a tinkling laugh. 'Don't forget the crusts!'

Jess went downstairs with her tongue out.

All morning Della had been dusting her bedroom and arranging things, but in the afternoon she brought her sewing down to the drawing-room, and Jess had to sit with her, and read aloud from the newspapers. She wanted to hear all the reviews of books, plays, exhibitions; then the editorial and gossip columns; lastly, and strangely, advertisements of houses, all rather grand, for sale – so that she could shake her head over the prices, and remark, 'Insane! If one were in that position, of having a look for a place—' Jess was used to smaller papers with bigger print. She wasn't in the habit of reading aloud, but Della was patient, and ready to correct her pronunciation if necessary; she sat with her back to the portrait of Sylvie, whose eyes, Jess thought, seemed to watch them scornfully from the moment they entered the room, and the making of the silk shirt proceeded, stitch by meticulous stitch. Jess longed to be outside, and slouched, and lost her place as she tried to stifle her yawns.

Della was aware – too aware – of her faults, and yet she found she couldn't help liking her. It was odd – yesterday she'd been appalled at her youth, and had accused Michael both in her mind and on the telephone of hiring the first unsuitable girl who answered his advertisement. But now, in that Indian thing, there was something reassuring about her unhurried movements, something calming in her presence. She didn't behave as if she had other things to do. There was a quality about her that Della couldn't easily identify, and misinterpreted as 'thick'. One would have to keep an eye on her – 'remember, you always draw curtains from the side' – as Jess, who had remembered, reached for the cord and closed them the required nine inches, so that the brilliant afternoon sunshine couldn't strike Della in the face. But she was restful to be with.

After tea there was a phone call from Josie.

'How's things?'

'So so.' Della was safely upstairs. 'You wouldn't like it.'

'Honest?'

'True. But it's okay. There's a pool, could you send on my costume?'

'Okay.' Grudgingly. 'Lucky pig. What chance do I get to swim? Mum never stops. She's on to me all day.'

'Is she all right?'

'*She* is. *I'm* not. Anyway I'm coming to see you and she can't stop me. I'll come for the day.'

'Could you get on and send the costume, so it comes before the weather breaks?'

'Is it hot with you?'

'It's lovely today. It's not raining with you, is it?'

'It might as well. There's no time even to look out the window. I'll let you know when I'm coming, or else I'll just turn up. Don't tell Mum.'

'You'd better, she'll go mad if you go off without telling her.'

'I'll tell Doc.'

'What's the good of that?'

'Why not, he's my father i'n't he?'

Jess was exasperated. 'Oh, grow up! Give them my love. Thanks for ringing. See you. Don't forget the costume.'

At nine-thirty she had another call.

'How's it going.'

'Oh. Okay, I think.'

'I haven't heard from Della, which must be a good sign.'

'She's gone to bed.'

'Are you still homesick?'

'I wasn't. I'd like to ring Mum sometime though, if you don't mind.'

'Why should I mind?' He sounded surprised.

'Cost, I was thinking,' she mumbled, embarrassed. Obviously he wouldn't notice the phone bill.

'Of course, ring her. Ring who you like, within continental limits that is.'

'How do you mean?'

'I'd sooner you didn't ring your boyfriend in Canada.'

'I haven't got one.'

'Not at all?'

'Not in Canada.' Her boyfirends were none of his business. There was a short silence.

'Della eats like a sparrow. I hope you're getting enough.'

'Oh yes, there's plenty here.'

'Have you decided what to give us next Friday?'

'Not yet.'

'Well, tell me if you want any specialities brought down from London.'

'*Specialities*?'

'I don't know – cumquats for instance. You won't find them in Palmers Cross.'

'Okay.' He had unnerved her with this unknown commodity.

'Goodnight, then,' he said.

'Goodnight.'

In London, Michael put down the telephone and walked to the window, to stare at the drab backs of the flats opposite. Lois, the girl who was sharing his supper and was obviously at home in his apartment, lifted the bottle and asked, 'More wine?'

'No, thanks.'

She poured another glass for herself. 'Cutting down?'

'No.'

'All well in the country?'

'Apparently.'

She studied his backview. The image she was at pains to achieve was fluffy blonde, but he had found out long ago that the fluff was superficial. Often he surprised a calculating expression in the big blue eyes.

'Why is it,' she said, as if she was thinking aloud, 'that drinking alone in front of you makes me feel so depraved?'

'Sylvie?' he suggested, dryly.

'Nothing to do with her! There's an unexpectedly puritanical side to you, darling. I think in a way you'd like to convert heathen, or thatch huts or something, instead of being a rich oil man.'

He wasn't interested in her speculations. He said, 'I went to Crouch End today.'

'What for?'

'To look at a pub.'

'No, Michael. You aren't up to that. Definitely not you. You don't even like beer.'

'I had a pint. Incognito. In the interests of research.'

'Really. What did you discover?'

'What did I discover,' he repeated, thoughtfully, still with his gaze sightlessly upon the concrete balconies and net curtained windows. 'I discovered that two and two don't inevitably make four, and that if you plant turnips you somethimes get – I don't know – a bunch of freesias__'

'What are you talking about?'

'A slob of a father, a shrew of a mother, a kid sister painted like a tart.'

'Charming!'

Six

Della slept soundly – Dr Burgess saw to that – but that night she dreamt of burglars, rapists and murderers, and tossed, moaning, until she managed to struggle awake in the grey dawn. Her nightgown was chilly with sweat against her skin. As she fumbled for her emergency pills, she knocked the little box flying and it rolled under the bed her heart fluttered, waiting to be transfixed by the ultimate pain, as she attached her trembling finger to the buzzer. Jess, roused in panic, half-fell out of bed, and hastened upstairs, pulling on her wrapper as she went. Della's head, turned towards her as she entered the bedroom, looked like a skull on the grey pillow in the grey light – a skull with glittering eyes.

'My pills – quickly!'

She dived for the box, and put it into Della's hand, gave her a drink. Once she had swallowed them, she became calmer. She lay back on the pillow with a sigh.

'Did you come up here during the night?'

'Me? No. No, I didn't.'

'I had this idea that there was someone in the room with me. Did you lock up?'

'Yes, of course,'

'Someone in my room, standing beside me, looking down at me with the most evil smile. I can't tell you how horrible it was. I'm not at all well Jessica, you must call the doctor, but not yet, it's early, but please don't leave me alone. Sit over there, where I can see you.' She twisted her head rapidly several times, moaned, and was silent. Jess sat in the place she had indicated. Her warm sleepiness had evaporated and she was thoroughly, coldly awake.

'I'm being a nuisance,' the moan came from the bed, after a while.

'No. It's no hardship sitting here.'

Della opened her eyes, and raising her head an inch, peered across at her. She closed them again, and lay back. Jess sat quite still, her anxious eyes fixed on the sheet as it rose and fell with Della's thin chest, in case it stopped moving. All round them the house seemed noisier than emptiness could possibly be – creaking stairs, and light footsteps across the ceiling. She could have sworn that an unseen hand pushed the bedroom door ajar. And she knew this was nonsense, logically she knew that Della had had a bad dream; but still she couldn't keep the grisly news items, that Josie revelled in, out of her mind. When six o'clock struck she leapt in her chair, it startled her so.

'Now you can telephone the doctor,' the invalid voice instructed. 'And Jessica – *don't bound.* It's so bad for my nerves.'

A visit from the doctor involved washing the face, brushing the hair, and a light application of scented powder. The nightdress and pillowslip had to be changed, and the curtains opened a fraction.

At last they heard a car crunch up the gravel and stop, the slam of a door. Jess going down to let him in, met him on the stairs. He was young, with curly brown hair.

She waited in the hall until he came down again, sooner than she expected. 'Would you like some coffee?'

'No I'll be getting back, thanks all the same.' He looked more closely at her and said, 'You're not the same girl.'

'I've only been here two days. Is she bad? Ought I to ring Mr Derby?'

'Lord bless you, don't bother *him*! She has these little turns. She'll have a quiet day, and be right as rain by tomorrow. Don't worry about her!'

He threw his case into the car and drove away. She watched from the steps until he was out of sight. Then she picked some roses and put them in a glass, and carried them up to Della. Dr Burgess had opened the curtains, and the room felt more optimistic.

Della said, 'I never have flowers in my room.'

'Why not?'

'Because flowers breathe out carbon dioxide, didn't you know that?'

'I'll take them away then.'

'No, no, you've picked them, they mustn't be wasted. Put them over there. It was a kind thought, and I shall enjoy looking at them.

Della with one of her little turns was even more demanding. Jess had to wait for her afternoon rest before she had a chance to ring home. As she stood by the telephone in the polished kitchen, she visualized in minute detail the culinary arrangements at the White Posts – the bottle gas with its horrible knack of running out before a function – the leaky wastepipe – the bit behind the back door which would never stay stuck down – the strip light that nobody got around to washing – the continuing threat of cockroaches, rats, and visits from 'the Health'. Her heart warmed to her mother, and to Doc, and Josie. She loved them dearly from this distance.

The feeling was evidently mutual, because Mum called her Pet, a name she mostly kept for Christmas and birthdays. As they talked, Jess made notes, as follows.

Proposed menu Friday night

STARTERS – prawn cocktails/avocadda vinegarette (if poss)/melon boats

Kejeree – bake your haddock flake into cooked rice don't over cook rinse in cold, stir in chopped hb eggs one each, heat in a big fry pan with oil/butter, sprinkle with chopped pars. Simple but watch rice

or

2 roast chickens should feed 6 if med large, stuff with packet, add chopped onion to gravy + chip soss & bits bacon veg roast or mash, froz peas carrots real or froz.

SALAD may not like mayenaise make vinegarette + garlic only if all like it

DESERT – chock mouse , bananna splits cheese & biscs

Her writing looked confident and covered two sheets of paper. She made some toast and a pot of jasmine tea, and carried it upstairs.

Della opened her eyes. 'How long have I been asleep?'

'About an hour. You nodded off while I was reading the paper.' She rearranged the pillows, and helped her on with her bedjacket. 'I brought you some tea and toast. You've had nothing all day.'

The room caught all the afternoon sunshine. Della sipped her tea. 'We had no summer at all until you came,' she observed. She bit into the toast. 'Tell me about yourself. Haven't you a sister?'

'Yes.'

'Older or younger? What's she called?'

'Josie. She's younger.'

'Do you get on well together?'

'Okay. Sometimes we fight. I suppose all kids do.'

'Mine didn't. I don't remember that Sylvie and Christian ever had a difference of opinion.'

This sentence, delivered like a judgement from the bed, had the effect of stopping the conversation.

'Does your mother work?' asked Della, after a silence.

'Yes. She cooks.' Jess could feel her face warming in anticipation of the next questions.

'You mean, for other people? As it might be, hotel work?'

'That sort of thing, yes.'

'And you help her, that's where you learnt to do – what was it – plaice in batter. People do eat such extraordinary things. Where did you train?'

'At home, I suppose,' mumbled Jess, but Della, to her surprise, approved of this.

'The best place. I had a girl come with qualifications a yard long, who couldn't so much as boil an egg, and the worst of it was, you couldn't tell her, because she took offence. Is your father in the catering business?'

'Yes, he is. Would you like more tea?' asked Jess desperately, lifting the lid of the teapot and peering in, to hide her blushes. 'I can easily add more hot.'

'No, my dear, I never drink hotted-up tea, but

thank you for your thought, and the toast, which was very nice. I think I'll get up for a little. I won't dress, I'll sit in my chair and look out at the garden, and perhaps do some sewing. No, don't worry – I can manage. You take the tray down.'

The sun was still warming the brick walls of the Bell House, and drawing the scents from the garden. As Della watched, a handful of rooks rose out of the wood behind the river, to float in the pinkish sky until the disturbance was past; when they subsided again among the trees.

Deeply soothed at last, she opened her workbox, and pulled the paper bag containing her sewing towards her. The carefully folded silk was not as she had left it. Her heatbeat quickened, her lips parted in a grimace, her eyes fixed on the shirt as she drew it from the wrapping into which it had been thrust. The exquisite stitching that fastened the right sleeve to the yoke had been roughly torn away, so that it dangled, like a broken arm.

Her face set in a mask of horror and distress. That was how Jess found her, with the sewing in her lap. Della had answered her knock automatically. She was yellow as wax, without any colour at all.

Seeing Jess, she made a pitiful effort to pull herself together. 'Isn't it silly,' she said, clearing her throat in the odd way she had. 'I tried to unpick this just now, and look what a mess I've made of it! I shall have to do it again!'

Jess discovered that Della had a larger appetite than she made out, particularly by night. Between Friday and Monday, the rest of the pâté, half a pound of butter and a packet of chocolate biscuits disappeared from the fridge, and only she could have taken them. Jess seemed to have heard that anorexics behaved like this. Perhaps she ought to mention it to the doctor; the fact that Della became almost hysterical when told that their food supplies were down, seemed to bear out her theory.

'All the chocolate biscuits?'

'An unopened packet.'

'And the *paté*! It seems such an odd combination; still, when you're young, you have a healthy appetite.'

There was no point in arguing about it. 'What sort of bathsalts do you want?' Jess was running her bath at the time.

'Mille fleurs, please.'

She threw them in, and scented clouds rose into the little bathroom; she came out, wiping her hands on her skirt.

'There's no butter left, or bread.'

'But I *can't* spare Mrs Drue on a Monday! Besides, she won't buy animal fats for moral reasons.'

'I can go, I'd like to go. It's not far to walk.'

'Well, perhaps, but you must let me think about it. I'll try to compose a list.'

Half an hour later, Jess walked out between the drive gates with a springy step and a light heart, carrying two baskets and a complicated list. On each side of the lane, behind thick hedges, real cows grazed, or raised their great heads to start as she passed. One relieved itself, with a noise like a bath tap. It was the closest she had ever come to cows. The lane was so overhung that the verges were still squashy in spite of three days' fine weather, and the hem of her skirt was damp through from the times she had to shrink against the hedge to let cars pass. (Mrs Drue was in one of them, and thus able, incognito, to have a good look at her.)

She had come this way in the taxi and it had taken five minutes, but now she walked for half an hour before she saw the iron sign at the bottom of the hill with PALMERS CROSS painted on it, PLEASE DRIVE CAREFULLY THROUGH OUR VILLAGE. At the top, she turned to look back. She could see the roofs of the Bell House, isolated in the distance, and follow from there the winding path of the hedge which marked the way she had come. All round, the farming landscape spread in gentle colours, green, brown and gold, with an occasional field of rape, so shockingly yellow, it looked as if God had spilt something.

Palmers Cross had never been rich or important, but recently townspeople had realized that it was within commuting distance, and the old properties were being snapped up and expensively refurbished. Men with educated voices played cricket on the green, and skittles in the Farmer's Arms. Their children went to school by car, because the village school and been closed long ago; the noticeboard advertised a disco. A home bakery, organic butcher and healthfood cum coffee shop had recently opened, though the original villagers – 'the natives', as they were jokingly called – still shopped as they always had, at the Stores, two old cottages with secretive little windows almost obscured by postcard advertisements. And Jess, attracted by their strangeness, called here first.

A bell pinged as she pushed open the door. Inside, the strip lights were on although it was a brilliant day, diffusing drabness over the shelves of goods ranging from groceries to pharmaceutical and hardware, everything you might want and yet when you asked for something it was often out of stock. The deep freeze was lollies and ice; the fruit looked as if it had travelled a long way. The floor space was cluttered with stands of postcards of other places, of gift wrap and newspapers and cheap stockings, as well as a few customers slowly coming to decisions. Opposite the door, at the far end of the shop, there was an illuminated cubicle with a window and counter, a post office evidently; a man with thinning grey hair and spectacles lurked inside, and looked Jess over as she came in.

She studied the other customers with lively interest. They were far stranger to her than people in a multi-racial city street. They all seemed much of an age, and wore the same kind of shapeless clothes, tied in at the waist. She wondered when, and where they had their hair done, to get that medium short, slightly frizzy style, of universal indeterminate browny-grey. When they spoke, she hardly expected to understand them, but it was English, the sort the TV interviewer discovers out in the sticks. They all seemed friendly together, but nobody so much as smiled at her.

An overalled person with lipstick and bobbed orange hair came through the bead curtain behind the till to serve her. She handed over what she wanted, which wasn't much, still conscious of the watery eyes of the post office keeper steadily observing her over the top of his glasses.

'Can you get fresh fish in the village?'

A hush fell, as if she'd asked for a video nasty. Jess glanced round, embarrassed.

'Only off of a van,' the grocer told her. 'What day is the fish this week, Arthur?'

'Tuesday,' Arthur intoned within his glass cubicle.

'Tuesday,' his wife repeated, as if Jess was deaf.

'Could you order me some haddock? Smoked, or smoked cod would do. Two bits, please.'

'He doesn't carry smoked, does he, Arthur?'

But Arthur seemed to think he might, so a large book was produced to write the order in. 'Name and address?' the orange-dyed woman, pencil poised inquired.

'It's for Mr Derby, at the Bell House.'

Suddenly, the shop was silent. Jess looked from the point of the woman's pen, up to her rapt expression, and so across to the gaunt man rigid like a cadaver in the glass-sided coffin of a post office compartment. The customers in the shop froze in their various attitudes, like children in the game Statues (who moves first is out).

Then the woman pulled herself together and wrote down the details, and Jess asked about vegetables.

'Over there, behind the postcards.'

'I mean, do you have any fresh? What I mean is, what day do you get them in?' She floundered under the grocer's outraged stare. 'Avocadder pears,' she said, desperately. 'Do you ever get avocadders?'

'Only Conference, and they're very nice, but not before October.'

After this Jess left the shop, conscious of every eye upon her. She turned her ankle and sat down heavily on the path, staining the back of her cotton skirt. She picked herself up, swearing under her breath, and remembered that she'd meant to buy a chocolate bar, but she certainly wasn't going back in there. She made for the pub, the Farmer's Arms, taking a short cut through the churchyard.

There were rooks in the tall old limes behind the

church. They had nested there for hundreds of years, witnesses through their ancestors of the first burials, whose inscriptions were illegible now on the tottering gravestones. They had seen the dead take over the ground, little by little, down to Mrs Grudge aged ninety-one, departed this life only three weeks ago, whose resting place was still brightly covered with flowers. Jess lingered, reading the messages – 'To darling Flo, from Stan' – what age could he be? Nice to be loved into your nineties! 'To our own precious Great Gran – Alison, Baby and the Twins.' The sharp eyes of the rooks had watched that grave over there being dug, a little apart from the rest. A lonely grave, that seemed somehow unreconciled, still expressive of grief in this peaceful place. She strolled over to look at it.

What she read on the stone made her catch her breath, and yet it was only one word. SYLVIE.

Sylvie was dead.

Oh horror! Oh poor Michael Derby!

There was nothing else to be learned from the stone, not even the date. At last she walked on.

Jess was a judge of pubs, and guessed this one sold more wine than beer. The man behind the bar was young and slim. He was polishing glasses without the telltale pint ready at his elbow. There were old beams and touches of polished copper in the right places, and a bowl of fresh flowers.

'What can I do for you?'

'Could I have a sandwich, please.'

'What sort do you want?'

'Cheese and chutney. White, please.'

He went away with the order, and she sat down at a table near the bar. Soon he came back.

'Where're you from?' he asked, conversationally.

'London.'

'On holiday are you?'

'I'm working near here.' She wondered how he would react to the name. She decided to try it. 'I work for Mr Derby at the Bell House.'

It meant little or nothing to him. 'Au pair girl, are you?'

'Cook.'

'You should have told me that when you ordered your sandwich,' he joked. It came through the hatch at that moment, and Jess took it greedily.

A shadow fell across her table as somebody passed the window, and a moment later, the door opened and an older man came in. There was a certain untidiness about him, an indefinable air of having been up till all hours, too busy to wash much, or change. A pipe and two cheap pens stuck out of his breast pocket. He sloped to the bar and ordered a pint, and then he turned and studied Jess. His eyes seemed to take her all in, and file her away under a label. She didn't like it, and didn't return his smile.

'She works at the Bell House,' said the barman, pushing across the brimming glass.

'Does she now,' said the man. 'You've overfilled it as usual, Sammy, it's not possible to drink clean at this bar.'

'Others would complain they weren't getting their money's worth.'

He shook his head without speaking, and took a swallow of beer; pulled out a rather grubby handkerchief and wiped his mouth and fingers; looked again at Jess. 'Mrs Fry well, I hope?'

'Not too bad,' she answered, with reserve.

'Is the boy at home?'

'No.'

'A treat in store. He's a handsome bugger.'

The man behind the bar said, 'Language Topper!'

'Language, what language? I've heard richer words than that in this bar. Not from a man, either. You'd have called her a lady, Sammy, but this was before your time. She had a very exceptional choice of words, very exceptional, and appreciated by me. She knew how to let her hair down of a Saturday night.'

Jess had the feeling that these remarks were aimed at her, without understanding why. The man called Topper made her uncomfortable.

'I don't agree with language, not in front of girls,' said Sammy, and he began to arrange his polished glasses.

'Girls! You should hear my Chloe!' Topper's Adam's apple jerked spasmodically as he gulped down the rest of his beer. Jess stood up and brushed the crumbs from her skirt. 'Have you got the right time, please?' she asked, directing her question pointedly at the barman.

'It's behind you. Five to twelve.'

She spun round. There was the clock and that was the time. And Della expected to eat at half past! Her face turned pink with fuss. She shoved back her chair and made for the door. How could she have been so careless? Lunch was going to be horribly late, even if she ran all the way.

She was crossing the street when she heard a shout behind her, 'You've forgotten your baskets!' She whipped round. Topper was standing outside the pub with one in each hand. As she ran back he said, 'Come on, I'll give you a lift. I'm going that way.'

It was a tatty, dirty little car, parked nearby. He opened the passenger door, and she crammed herself in. It smelt of newspapers and tobacco; there were a lot of old newspapers on the back seat, and the ashtray was stuffed with fag ends.

'Thanks a lot.'

'Don't mention it. Don't flinch, I'm not feeling for your knee, I'm trying to change gear.'

She moved her leg. He pulled out and said, 'How long have you been at the Bell House?'

'Since Friday.'

'You've met him of course.'

'Who?'

'Michael Derby.'

'Yes'

'Charming?'

'Is he?'

He's rich enough anyway.'

She said nothing, and Topper didn't speak again until he stopped by the drive gate. Then he said, out of the blue, 'Watch your step with glamour boy Michael. He could be very bad news.'

He had dropped his bantering tone, and was looking her in the face, as if trying to gauge the impression his words had made. She clambered out of the car. 'Thanks for the lift.'

He raised his hand and backed into the driveway, returned in the direction of the village. She understood then that the Bell House hadn't been on his way; he had wanted to warn her.

Della was sowing by the drawing-room window, but neither waved nor smiled. A mop flourished from her bedroom just as Jess reached the front door, and Mrs Drue herself descended on the dot of twelve-thirty. Jess looked round from the stove with a very red face, as she had completely forgotten about the cleaning lady (my own choice, dear, and not what I've been used to, but it brings in a little welcome pocket money).

'Now you mustn't bother about me,' she said at once, divining that she had not been included in the menu. 'Mrs Fry should have warned you that I always bring my own haybag—' here she laughingly produced certain brown substances wrapped in clingfilm. She came up behind Jess and bending her head close, whispered to make it a secret between them, 'Vegetable solids barely interrupt the ecto-plasmic flow.'

This was Greek to Jess. 'There's a tin of veg soup,' she suggested.

'Not for me! I couldn't touch it!' Mrs Drue nodded and smiled and shook her head, and all through lunch repeated these movements whenever she caught Jess's eye, or formed inaudible words with her lips.

Della was edgy and critical during lunch, destruct-ive to the ectoplasmic calm of the kitchen.

'Did you remember Mrs Grabham's nice eggs?'

'They only had the supermarket kind, I didn't get them.'

'That's very surprising! Sometimes on a Monday they aren't quite fresh, but they always have them, in a little basket by the door. But you got the honey?'

'There wasn't any.'

'Oh, Jessica, there *must* have been! You didn't look properly.'

'They had the usual, produce of more than one country. There wasn't any local.'

'But they *never* stock that horrid stuff! Are you *sure*?'

'Yes.'

Della thought it over, forking at her omelette discontentedly. Mrs Drue winked and mouthed.

'You did *go* to the Coffee Shop?'

'No.'

'But, Jessica!' in a wail. 'They are the people who sell the eggs and honey! I suppose you only looked in that horrid General Stores. There's nothing in that place fit for human consumption.'

'I'll call in on my way here tomorrow, Mrs Fry – no, that's a little fib, because it *isn't* on my way here; but I'll certainly call in tomorrow morning for you, without any trouble at all.'

Della had to be grateful, against her will because she was in a bad temper, and declining cheese, left the table early.

Jess was dogged by Mrs Drue, standing by the sink like a monument, smilingly polishing pans with a dry cloth. Her hands were large, and smooth because she always worked in gloves. Her skirt bagged where she sat, and her jersey, of pink knitting in a lacy pattern, though not nice, would have looked better on a younger woman. Her straight white hair was bobbed in a style that reminded Jess of the cardinals in a picture they had at White Posts, drinking together round a table and called *The Spirit of Good Cheer*. Mrs Drue's cheerful spirit exuded from every inch of her. Jess doubted whether anything would shift it, even her full weight on the sandalled foot; she was tempted to try.

Della kept to her bedroom with the door shut. The buzzer was silent. Jess took the opportunity to write letters.

Bell House
Palmers +
Dolchester

Dear Rache

Sorry not to have written but have been on the go a lot, not hard work, but not much free time either. Hope you're well & the salon, are you cutting yet, tell your Mum she ought to move down here, I walked to the village this a.m. & its quite a dump, ok its pretty but the women I saw aren't or friendly either. Anyway I got given a lift back here by this bloke so that was human, but he's not my type or yours either, older than Doc for a start.

When are you off abroad? Dont forget to send pc of sun, beach, tanned bodies ect. hope you can read address on this.

You might go up to W.P. if you get a minute, I hope Mum's ok but she doesn't get time to write, its funny I miss her more than any of them. Tell Josie from me to get down to it if she's not. Tell them I don't like using the phone but they can ring here.

Theres this weirdo does the cleaning ect she told me she sees her husband every Friday 6.30 pm why not I hear you ask but the fact is he's been dead 4 years! Says she often sees ghosts & looks like she could tell me things she's seen here but I dont want to know. Mrs Fry who lives here is a NOCTURNAL & thats enough for me. She nicks things out of the fridge & then tells me what a big appetite I've got. Another weirdo! Still I'm glad I came its a lovely place, my room you wouldn't believe!! Colour TV (haven't watched it yet) & own bathroom, shower, biday. Gadgets in kitchen like waste disposal unit Mum could do with (put Josie in it) veg peeler that works self clean ovens ect. I've got to do a Dinner Friday night so keep your fingers + d. I like being in the country its nice once you get used to the quiet, tennis court & pool* in garden, bit of a waste with nobody to use them but MD** down this w.e. & bringing friends so I shall See Life.

You might look up Mum for me.

All my Love,

Jess X

*Tell Josie to send costume if she hasnt

**Gave interview

By the same post she sent Josie a view of Palmers Cross, which had been in the Stores so long that it was priced in old money.

Hope you sent costume weather still brilliant hope all well at home take care love to all let me know if youre coming love Jess X

Della continued overcast. She was particularly peevish about Friday's dinner, Jess discovered.

'Since you and Michael have organised this between you, of course it's not for me to say, I shan't express an opinion because as far as I'm concerned, I'm not involved. I never participate in this sort of entertainment, I hardly know his friends. All the same I do think it's just a little thoughtless of him, to throw a dinner party, when you've only been here a few days, and after all he's no idea of your capabilities. It's not that I doubt you, Jessica, but a little consultation beforehand might perhaps have been wise. Michael can be very demanding. You have to remember that he's very travelled, very sophisticated; his standards are high. He expects a great deal, and he can be outspoken, unkind even, if he doesn't get it.'

Jess feared, as well as hated her, as she sat very upright, clearing her throat now and then in punctuation of this speech, her large brown eyes slightly bloodshot, braced and motionless apart from the movements of her full lips. She explained, 'It's just that I have to shop for Friday, and I don't know what the markets are round here. The village Stores don't have much.'

'It would be odd if they did. I don't suppose they've even heard of the sort of thing Michael expects to eat.' A pause – a thrust, in the blandest tone. 'What are you going to give them?'

'I thought melon, or avocadders to start with.'

'Ah-doe's, Jessica. Nothing to do with snakes. You certainly won't find them at Palmers Cross. What's your main course?'

She'd ordered the fish, so there was no need to risk the word kedgeree. 'I need a couple of chickens.'

'What, an Emincés de Volaille perhaps? or Poulet à l'Estragon? For chicken you really can't do better than the butcher in Palmers Cross; you should have ordered them this morning.'

'I can walk up tomorrow.'

'Well, but perhaps it won't suit me that you are away again for half the day. I may need you here. And while we're on the subject, Mrs Drue tells me that you had a lift back with Sid Topper. Is he a friend of yours?'

'No.'

'Where did you meet him?'

Oh God. 'He saw I was in a hurry. He said he was coming this way.'

'I don't know why he should have been.' The lips moved, the eyes were fixed, but the face was somehow darker, as if Della was upset for some reason. She went on, 'You oughtn't ever to take lifts from strangers, surely you know that. Sid Topper works for the *Dolchester Chronicle*. He is a representative of what I would call the gutter press, people like him delight in making trouble for decent folk, with half-truths and preconceived opinions. If he offered you a lift, you can be sure he had an ulterior motive.' She paused, hoping for a reaction from Jess; then with a sigh continued, 'Well, whatever you said, it's too late now. – If you want chickens delivered by Friday, you'll have to order them today.'

Jess moved thankfully towards the door.

'But wait a minute! They're shut on Monday afternoons. Well, you'll have to catch them first thing tomorrow, but I'm afraid you've left it too late. They certainly won't have time to pluck them.'

'If it's just the delivery, Mrs Drue could bring them out.'

Della shook her sewing, selected a needle. 'Mrs Drue won't handle meat of any sort, even in a wrapper,' she said. 'She's very sensitive about it.'

With which annihilating swipe the interview was closed. One way and another, Jess wasn't surprised when the telephone rang at half past nine.

'How are things?'

She knew that it was bound to be him, and still his voice took her by surprise.

'Oh. Okay.'

'You sound a bit tired.'

'I'm okay.'

'Della being difficult?'

She longed to say, 'Vile.' 'A bit,' she said.

'You're cagey. Have you had a row?'

'No.'

'Given in your notice?'

'No.'

'Good, because I'm going to Stavanger tomorrow, and if you're going to have a crisis I want to know about it.'

'It isn't a crisis.'

'I'm glad to hear it.' Pause. 'Do you know where Stavanger is?'

'No.'

'Norway. I'm back on Friday and I'll come straight down, I should make it by seven. The guests won't arrive before eight. We'll dine at half past, quarter to nine.'

Dine. 'Do you—'

'What's the matter?'

'Is chicken all right roasted?'

'Why shouldn't it be? We had it tonight, very good it was.'

'I hope you have a good trip.'

'Thanks. Don't get downhearted. She's always a bit on edge after a turn.'

'Okay.'

She put down the phone. She imagined that he had been calling from a hotel bedroom. The other half of 'we' lay on the bed in a black lace nightgown and scarlet négligée frilled down the front; she was very slim, with long legs and long black wavy hair. Oddly enough, he was fully dressed, though he had loosened his pure silk designer tie. He had been talking on a white telephone but there was a red and a black one on the executive desk which her imagination somehow fitted into the bedroom, as well as a leather-bound diary full of engagements with his monogram in gold in one corner. While Jess watched, he reached for his cigar box (also monogrammed), extracted one, lit it and inhaled, indolently. The girl on the bed stretched out one arm to him but he ignored her, strolling instead to the window to stare down into the street with its fluorescent lighting and pleasure-seeking throng. He was thinking about his work. 'Michael—' the girl said, plaintively. 'No,' he replied, the syllable firm, decisive. 'I have to pack.' There was a leather suitcase open on the huge desk and he began throwing in his things, careless, expensive. Outside the jets were streaming to and fro along the pitch-black flight path between Heathrow and Stavanger.

Seven

Jess had never plucked a chicken in her life.

It was Friday morning, and she had just unpacked the butcher's bag. She stared at the contents with dismay and panic in her breast – their heads and necks, and dreadful claws— – Mrs Drue came into the kitchen, and cast a pitying look at the table.

'I never know how you meat-eaters can reconcile it to yourselves,' she remarked.

'But what happened?' wailed Jess. 'I asked for them to be cleaned!'

'Cleaning is gutting, not plucking.'

Jess was desperate. 'You couldn't – you wouldn't do them for me?'

'Not for a thousand pounds – not for ten thousand! I could never square it with my conscience.'

Jess moved them to the sink, and turned on the cold tap. Two hours later, with a sickened heart, she hid the result in the crisp tray and pushed it into the fridge. Luckily she'd prepared everything she could the day before, but when she looked at the mousse, she discovered to her fury that Della had been on one of her midnight raids, and three of the little glass bowls were empty. She felt very angry about this, particularly because the dirty dishes had been left in the fridge. Fortunately she'd made a dozen.

Mrs Drue opened the door to the doctor. Whenever

Michael entertained, Della fortified herself with medical attention. By the time Jess carried up an experimental helping of kedgeree, she was dressed, and sitting wanly in her chair.

'I thought you might like to try some of this, we're having it tonight,' she said, carefully setting down the tray on the table beside her.

Della stared with a certain hostility at her plate, and unfolded her napkin with a sigh. 'You'll help with Roz's room, won't you? I wanted to do it myself. I like to add the little touches, a few flowers, fresh biscuits in the tin – Roz is a very old friend, and rather special.'

Jess was leaving the room when she added, 'I don't want to be a nuisance today of all days when you've so much to do, and you mustn't dream of labouring up here with plates of what you're giving them for dinner. I couldn't possibly digest all that. Just a simple little supper is all I need – one of your nice plain omelettes, and a cup of clear soup with toast.'

'Would you like some chocolate mousse?' asked Jess, pointedly.

'No, thank you. I shall be happy thinking of everyone else enjoying it. And, Jessica,' as she was closing the door, 'always *brown* rice—'

For Roz the suite of rooms across the landing had been opened. Jess took up a vase of hastily arranged flowers, interested to look inside. Mrs Drue was there, polishing the already gleaming surfaces. The room was beautifully and comfortably furnished, and yet it had a disused, melancholy air.

'Was this Mrs Derby's room?'

'That's right.'

Jess could imagine the girl in the picture choosing

a frock from the fitted cupboard, eyeing herself critically in the glass; waking up in the wide, glamorous bed.

'She was Sylvie to me. Sweet Sylvie. Many's the time I've sat up here with her, when she was taken poorly. She didn't like her brother to see her then, but she never minded old Droobie. The hours I've spent with her in this very room, holding her hand, listening to her stories.'

'What stories?'

'Now you're asking me to break the confidences of the sick room, which is something I could never, never do. But I told her how it would be. You see, I knew her before they married, it was me opened up the house for them to look at.' Mrs Drue's big hands were folded on the duster, the moist moons of her eyes were lost in reminiscence. The low pitch of her voice somehow added to the urgency of her narrative.

'He went striding on into the different rooms. I said to her (and remember, she was a stranger,) my dear, I said, there's more to life than feather beds, oysters and champagne. The cage may be gilded but it is still a cage. But he was very tempting, and she fell. Have you a brother?'

'No.'

'My Sylvie and her Christian were very close – hand in glove, you might say. That's the sadness of it. For she'd have never have hurt a hair of his head – oh, she'd have killed anyone who tried! And when she died, he was dreadfully affected. He was like a wild beast with the shock of it. I don't know how many specialists he had to be taken to, and you have to admit it, Mr Derby was very good like that, not that the boy ever thanked him for it. No, he hated him then and— ' Mrs Drue was suddenly silent. Jess looked round. Della was standing in the doorway, a thin, admonitory figure.

'I thought I heard voices. I've finished with my tray, Jessica, if you'd like to take it down.'

Jess returned to the kitchen. She prepared plenty of bacon and sausages, to disguise the not entirely perfect appearance of the birds, and arranged the stuffing round them in balls. She peeled the vegetables, put out the prawns to thaw, cut the melons into quarters and made them into boats with coloured spills from the drawing-room and paper sails. It took a while to do this, but she thought they looked pretty. The kedgeree was ready to heat, and Della hadn't complained about it, so it must be fairly all right. It was unexpectedly difficult to halve the avocados, and almost impossible to extract the stones without smashing the flesh, but she did her best. The flesh itself had black bits, but she supposed this was normal. The banana splits were easy, she'd often made them. Worst of all would be the laying of the table, but she didn't intend to tackle that until Mrs Drue had gone home, so she filled in the time by writing out a couple of menus, using black felt-tip and curly letters – they looked quite artistic.

At four o'clock she hurried into the dining room. She'd found a glass dish in the shape of a waterlily for the melon boats, and they looked lovely in the centre of the table. Six polished wine glasses contained peeled prawns nestling in the best bits of the lettuce on a bed of mayonnaise, while the avocados were arranged on a plate round the vinaigrette handy in a bottle, the smallest empty she could find, so that people could shake their own – this was a dodge of

Mum's, appreciated by the customers at the White Posts. She folded the paper napkins into elaborate shapes, and put them on the waterlily side plates that matched the dish in the middle. There were rather a lot of knives and forks, because of the choice of food, but she expected these guests would be able to find their way among them, and they looked lavish. All the cruets were out on the table, shining like little suns, filled with fresh salt and pepper and different mustards, and there was a choice of sugars in more dazzling silver. She put the cheese biscuits in some silver containers she found on the dresser, like bowls, but with straight sides, and the cheese lay on a flowery plate with a basin over it to stop it from drying out. She added glasses for wine, and the menus. Then she paused, looking it all over, moving a salt cellar a fraction to the left, putting the serving spoons in pairs. The colours of the spills had run into the melon, but it was hardly noticeable, and probably not toxic. On the whole, she was pleased. It looked lovely, and she wished she had a camera, to take a picture of it for Mum.

Della buzzed loud and long. Jess flew, cursing, upstairs, and opened the door more abruptly than usual.

'How are you getting on?'

'Okay.'

'I don't like to carp, Jessica, but I do prefer the Queen's English to American.'

But Jess saw that Della was holding a turquoise blue silk scarf with a delicate pattern on it – very beautiful it was – she was holding it out to Jess.

'I came on this the other day and I thought it would suit you, I'd like you to have it.'

Jess bent her blushing face over it, mumbled her thanks. 'It's lovely. It's really nice of you. I love it.'

'It's a little thank you present, because you've been kind. Thank you, my dear.' She turned back to her chair, upright, strained, difficult. Jess's eyes blurred with sudden tears. 'It's really nice of you,' she said again.

Now the chickens were in, the vegetable water on, the kedgeree heating slowly. The salad was washed and dried, and one clove of garlic lay questioningly on the table. Jess had a shower, and tied back her hair with the scarf which matched her dress exactly. It was almost seven. She went into the drawing-room which had a soft glow at this time of day, without artificial lights. Mrs Drue had arranged two bowls of roses, and their scent mixed with the multiple scents wafting in through the open windows. Jess stood in the middle of the room and stared up at Sylvie – Droobie's pet. She wondered in what way she had been poorly. She looked full of health and vitality.

She heard a movement, and spun round. Michael Derby had come in behind her.

'You've lost weight,' he said. 'I thought you would. You look well, though.'

He had forgotten that she was beautiful. Beneath the poised, society portrait, beneath that girl who had brought so much grief into his life, she seemed to him to stand like an angel, with a fiery innocence that for some reason disturbed his heart.

Jess's cheeks were flaming with embarrassment. 'I didn't hear you arrive.'

'We went up the back drive. Roz has gone up to say hello to Della. I want a bath. Is everything under control?'

'I think so.'

'It smells good. I'd better open some wine.'

'Jessica!' a female voice called from upstairs.

Roz was tall and slim, and looked good in trousers. Her hair however was not long and black, but brown, cut short and curly round her face.

'I'm Roz. Hallo,' she said, shaking hands while Jess was still one step below. 'Della wants you.' She led the way into the bedroom.

'Roz says it's too cold for me in here. Could you close the windows? And turn down my bed, then I shan't have to bother you later. And my dressing gown—– Not the blue one, the black with the Chinese birds. And the black velvet slippers. Thank you, Jessica.' Jess noticed that Roz was watching Della in the amused, indulgent way she might have looked at a spoilt child. Della added, 'I like the scarf in your hair. It's pretty, worn like that.'

'All dressed up for the party,' said Roz. She spoke kindly. Jess hated her. She almost collided with Michael as he came into the bedroom. She hurried downstairs, in a fluster.

Later, when she returned to the bedroom with Della's supper on a tray, he was there; he had changed his clothes, and bathed presumably. As she came in he was saying, 'I shouldn't worry about it.' He glanced at her and held up the silk shirt Della was making against himself. 'A perfect fit,' he said, in a different sort of voice. 'Isn't there a fairy story about a shirt with only one sleeve?'

'Jessica can tell us,' said Della. 'She is closer to her childhood than we are .'

But Jess didn't know it. He removed the sewing things from the table so that she could place the tray.

For a moment his sunburnt hands were close to her white ones. His were strong, bony, with slim fingers and flat, oval nails; hers still had a childish softness. He glanced from her hands to her face, but she didn't meet his eyes. Her cheeks were unusually pink.

All three paused, listening, as a powerful car crawled up the gravel. It stopped just below. Michael moved to the window and looked down.

'The Carters,' he told them in a low voice. 'Odd, seeing them from up here – I didn't realize he was so bald. I'd better go down. Enjoy your supper,' he said to Della, touching her shoulder as he passed her chair. 'We'll eat at nine,' he told Jess. He went out and they heard his quick feet on the stairs, his welcoming voice, 'Bill and Di! Good to see you—' etc, etc, the sound effects dwindling as they moved together onto the terrace.

Jess went down by the back stairs. She was straining the peas when he strode in and took a bottle out of the fridge. She asked timidly, 'Will everyone like garlic?'

'Good God, I don't know! You'd better ask them!'

She buttered the peas and sprinkled them with sugar, and put them in the oven to keep warm. Then, holding onto her courage, she walked out onto the terrace. Michael had stuck some wax torches into the flowerbeds which burnt with a glamorous light and a subtle scent that was meant to discourage bugs. Roz was looking wonderful in a skin-tight, low-cut brown dress, that would have made Jess look like a parcel; Michael, very close to her, was pouring her a glass of wine. All the guests had arrived and were talking or laughing, but everyone paused as Jess appeared, and looked in her direction. She said, 'Excuse me, but do you all like garlic?'

There was a disconcerted silence. Michael frowned. Roz said, 'Yes, I'm *sure* we all do,' and smiled up at him. Nobody contradicted her, and Jess escaped thankfully, as a man called Simon began a long story about its usefulness as an aphrodisiac in remote bits of Catalonia. She made the salad and then she was ready, but it was well after nine before they moved into the dinning-room.

She waited with a palpitating heart for their reactions. There was silence at first, and then some remarks – she couldn't hear what was said. Several people laughed. She heard the scraping of chairs as everyone sat down, and the door was shut. She stood in the kitchen and timed them ten minutes for the starters. Then she took a pad and pencil, and crossed the hall. There was something horribly daunting about the closed door, and it seemed unnaturally silent inside. She hesitated, dreading the general stare, wanting the conversation to begin again before she entered. She heard Michael say, 'She seems to suit Della, anyhow,' and her face flamed. She knocked, and went in, and started round the back of the chairs collecting the dirty plates. Roz seemed to feel she had to help, which was irritating. Simon groped for her knee as soon as she moved within reach.

'What's the pad and pencil for?' said Michael, as she waited at the opposite end of the table.

'Who wants fish, and who chicken,' she replied.

'Good gracious!' said the woman called Di, with a silly laugh. The other guests were looking at Jess. It dawned on her that they thought she was funny.

Michael said, 'I should serve the fish, and then we can go on to the chicken.' He didn't sound amused. She'd forgotten to bring in a tray, so it took two journeys to clear the table.

The kedgeree didn't seem popular. Poor Jess served the chicken with an anxious heart. It looked all right. But as she was leaving the room, the fat woman on Michael's left, whose name was Patricia, said plaintively, 'I'm not sure I like knowing what colour the bird was that I'm eating,' as she held up a bedraggled brown feather. And as she shut herself into the kitchen, she heard a sudden shout of laughter.

There was a young man in the kitchen. He was standing between the table and the fridge. He was holding a bowl of that ill-fated chocolate mousse, and as she gazed at him, struck dumb, he ran his finger round the inside of it and licked off the last, boldly returning her stare. His eyes were deep blue and he had curly light brown hair, rather long, and uncombed.

She didn't speak but went straight to the fridge and flung open the door. There were four banana splits left, and three little dishes of mousse. She turned on him furiously, but her heart was cold with despair.

'I'm afraid I have what you call a sweet tooth,' he remarked. His voice was soft, apologetic. He gave her a crooked little smile. 'You shouldn't be such a good cook.'

She began loading the dishwasher with quick, nervous movements – she'd have recognized her mother at once, if she could have seen herself objectively. She could have cried with fuss. The meal was a disaster. She put the remaining puddings on a tray and carried them into the dining-room, and started to clear the table. The company looked pretty merry. There were several empty wine bottles on the dresser. The boy had followed her as far as the doorway.

'Is that you, Christian?' said Micahel, catching sight of him. 'Sit down, Roz,' he added impatiently, putting his hand on her arm, 'he can give Jess a hand. Here Jessica—' his eyes were very bright, his face red, but no one would have ignored the summons. 'Do you know what this is?' and he handed her a plate, with two soggy little parcels on it. 'No.' Well, have a look at them. *In the kitchen*, not here.' She wanted to sink through the floor, without knowing why he was displeased. Patricia said, in an unnatural tone, '*I* think she's done *very well*,' and Simon started a long story about the use of chicken hearts in the treatment of unmentionable diseases in the foothills of the Himalayas.

Bill had made paper darts of the menus and was wearing them behind his ears, behaviour that would have been frowned on at the White Posts. She put the cheese and biscuits on the table, said pitifully, without meeting Michael's eyes, 'I hope you're enjoying your meal,' and fled. Christian was sitting moodily by the kitchen table.

'I'm sorry, but I don't see why I should help wash up. I assume you're paid to do it, and I'm not. Is there anything more to eat?'

'Kedgeree. Or you can have all these.' She pushed the plate of avocados towards him.

'I don't like them. What's up with Michael? He sounds a bit sharp.'

'I don't know.' With trembling hands she was undoing one of the little oily parcels. It contained the giblets of the bird, baked to an ugly purple.

'Guts,' said Christian, simply. 'You forgot to take them out. Can you make cakes?'

'There's no one to eat them.'

'There is now. I could spend more time at home now you're here. Droobie used to do it, but she gave all that up when she became a vegan. Do you know about Sylvie?' He asked the question without any difference in his voice, any change in the expression of his eyes.

'Yes. You might grind me some coffee beans.'

'I don't know how to work the machine. Who told you? Not Michael, I bet, he never mentions her.'

Jess chucked the kedgeree and the avocado pears into the waste disposal unit and switched it on. She switched on the coffee bean grinder. The whirring of machinery killed conversation. She carried the coffee tray into the drawing-room, and opening the dining-room door said, 'Your coffee has now been served.' As she closed the door she heard Simon's fat voice, 'Oh go on, Michael, get her in, let's have some fun. There's one or two questions I'm dying to ask her,' and his reply, barely civil, 'Die, then; she isn't a side show.'

Jess went upstairs to Della, who had gone to bed. The nightlight was dim and kind. She collected the supper tray.

'Thank you, Jessica. It's being a success, I can tell. I never heard so much laughter! I daresay they'll make a night of it. Well, it's good for Michael to enjoy himself. I can rest all day tomorrow. Goodnight, my dear.'

Christian passed her on the landing. 'I'm tired. I'm going to bed now.' He went on up the next flight of stairs, to the attic studio which had been made for

Sylvie. As he disappeared round the bend in the staircase, the ladies Roz, Di and Patricia emerged from Roz's bedroom where they had been repairing their hairstyles and make-up. They had been chattering and giggling like girls, but stopped when they saw Jess with the invalid tray. There was a certain dignity about her, as she waited for them to go first downstairs, that caused Di to murmur, 'I don't quite see what we could have done—' before they joined the gentlemen in the convivial drawing-room.

The dining-room was a wreck, the chairs covered with crumbs and wine dripping from the table on to the carpet. An extraordinary number of glasses and plates seemed to have been used. The dishwasher began its cleaning and polishing routine, filling the kitchen with its discreet hum. The party was now shut in the drawing-room, but from time to time one of the gentlemen erupted in the direction of the downstairs cloakroom, and by and by Jess heard a heavy tread in the hall, and realized that someone was coming her way. The kitchen door opened and Simon stood there staring round, dazzled at first by the fluorescent lighting.

Jess drenched the cloth she was using in cold water; she knew he was drunk; if he thought that kissing the au pair was included in the evening's entertainment, he was in for a nasty surprise. But he had more expertise than the fumblers at the White Posts. He came up lightly and speedily behind her, and jamming her against the sink with his heavy body, buried his boozy face in her hair. She trod as hard as she could on his foot, and slapped at his face with the cloth but got most of the cold water down her own neck. 'Little bitch,' he mumbled passionately. 'Wonderful, wonderful girl—' at the same time catching hold of her wrists in a vice-like grip. She jerked back her head and got him on the nose, and that must have hurt because he swore. 'Come here, you—' he muttered, evil purpose thickened by alcohol. 'Don't pretend you've never been kissed, with eyes like you've got—'and he began wrenching her round, using her body and legs to pinion her against the sink. The electric kettle fell with crash and tepid water splashed across the floor. Nothing she could do, or say, had the slightest effect on him; he intended to get what he wanted, and her struggles made him more determined. 'Playing hard to get,' he said hoarsely into her ear. 'Okay, little girl, if that's the way you want it—'

The winey fumes of his breath reached her face. She grimaced, sickened, disgusted. He was muttering, 'The tough ones are always the sweetest,' with his horrible blubbery lips feeling for her skin – when there was suddenly a noise like a pistol shot, and he fell away, so abruptly that she nearly lost her own balance. She leant back, gasping against the kitchen table, rubbing her arms, her breath coming quick and hard; while in front of her Simon picked himself up from the floor, grunting, and scarlet in the face. Michael was filling a glass with water. Simon drank several mouthfuls, and put it down without a word. He didn't look at Jess as he stumbled out of the kitchen, but Michael said, in a chilly tone, 'I must apologize for the behaviour of my guests.' Then he shut the door behind them.

There were puddles and footmarks all over the floor. She cleared it up, and then went into her own room and bolted the door, for the first time in her life. She sat on the side of the bed, shivering and crying. At last she pulled herself together and found one of the old postcards she'd bought at the shop and wrote to warn Mum. 'Dinner total failure all things vile sure to get sack all love JX' There was a letterbox close by, in the lane, and she went out straightaway to post it. As she was turning back into the drive, she saw that they were all leaving. Roz and Michael were standing together in the lit doorway, cars were revving and cheery remarks were being exchanged. If she stayed in the lane she would be seen, and she had to cross the drive to reach her room by the back way. So she shrank among the bushes, and nobody saw her, not even Simon in the front passenger seat beside Patricia, staring out with a glassy expression. By now Roz had disappeared into the house, and Jess expected Michael to shut the door and turn off the lights. But after all he must have caught a glimpse of her, for after a moment's hesitation, he stepped foward and called in a low voice, 'Jessica?'

This was it, then, this was the sack. All the expectations and hopes, all the patience and effort – because she had tried, and she had kept her temper with Della – rose in her breast, choked her with misery at the injustice of it. She stayed where she was, biting her thumbnail, ready to swear, or weep, feeling somehow exposed as if Simon's paw marks were visible. Michael began walking down the garden towards her. But sensitive to her distress, he stopped halfway, and said again, questioningly, 'Jess?'

She came out then. Her dark dress blotted into the

midnight garden. But her face and hair, her arms were silver.

'You aren't running away, are you?'

'No.'

'Are you very upset?'

'I'm okay.'

'What's *okay*? You're always saying it. I don't know what you mean by this word.'

They stood in the darkness, close enough to touch but not touching. Roz in the act of drawing her bedroom curtains would not have spotted them, except that a car in passing down the lane caught them fractionally in the beam of its headlights.

'I'm sorry about Simon.'

She nearly said, 'That's okay,' again, but stopped herself. Instead she said, 'He's immature, that's all.' It sounded a pathetic excuse. She added, 'You can't be responsible for your friends.'

'That's a rather cutting remark.'

Roz wondered what on earth they could be up to down there.

'He's not a friend,' he added, after a silence. 'Sylvie – my wife – had these fans. I've kept on with them because – I don't know, if you have a country house you somehow have a social round. At least, I feel you ought to. You might be a bit lonely otherwise.'

Another silence. Roz watched them moving slowly back towards the house. She thought of joining them, but she was about to have her bath.

'The river sounds clearer at night than it does in the day,' said Michael.

'We've got a clock like that at home,' Jess told him, shyly.

'I'd have sold the place long ago if it hadn't been for the river. What sort of clock?

'I don't know. Just the ordinary sort. Doc keeps it ten minutes fast.'

'Who's Doc?'

'Dad.'

He stood back on the threshold so that she could pass first into the house: close enough to touch, but not touching.

Roz opened her bedroom door as he came on to the landing. She had taken-off her make-up and brushed her hair. He knew that she was naked under her dressing gown.

'Did you manage to comfort the poor kid?'

'I suppose so.'

'Don't sound so *down*, darling! Simon's incapable of hurting anyone. Maybe he even gave her morale a boost – after that rather disastrous meal!'

'Oh rubbish,' said Michael.

He went into his room. She looked after him, surprised. The door was ajar, she noticed, but she knew better than to follow him. Let him come to her – and he would – if not now, in the morning.

On the floor above, Christian lay on his back and stared at the ceiling. There was a divan in the studio, but he was lying on a pile of old clothes, skirts and blouses and sweaters all belonging to Sylvie, that he had pulled out of her cupboards and drawers and heaped higgledy-piggledy in a corner.

The chill moon peering round the window frame like an eavesdropper, fingered the Chinese screen, the exercise bicycle, the baby grand, ran its lengthening eye along the looking glass, before drawing out in shades of grey the different dyes of those tumbled clothes, and painting with silver brightness the young man's face. Still he lay, open-eyed, and even his closest friend – if he had one – couldn't have guessed what was on his mind.

Eight

'The whole art of a dinner is organization quite honestly,' Roz said next morning. It was nine o'clock and she was already beautiful in a crisp blouse, and perfectly tailored trousers that showed off her long, slim legs. Even her toenails, poking out of the kind of sandals one could only find abroad, were polished. Her gleaming hair smelt faintly of apples. Jess on the other hand, to whom she was addressing this information, still wore her Indian wrap; she had just spent an hour with Della. She had washed her face and brushed her teeth and hair before she went up, but about her large form there still clung an indefinable, peaceful aura of sleep. It annoyed Roz. Roz annoyed Jess: after all, she was not yet Mrs Derby.

'You have to decide what you can do really well, and make that your main course. Starters and puddings are easy, anyone can knock up a mousse or a prawn cocktail – I think this kettle must be broken.' She looked at it more closely. 'It's dented as well. It looks as if it's been dropped.'

'I'll boil some water in a saucepan.'

'Did you drop it?'

'No. What do you want for breakfast?'

'Oh – nothing. Just coffee and toast – I can get it. Where was I? Yes, you need a strong main course, and quite honestly *not* roast chicken because even if it's good, it's really not clever enough. If that's for me, I don't take milk in coffee. Yes, that's masses of toast, thanks. No, I never eat butter – just a smear of marmite. As I was saying, I think quite honestly the mistake you made last night was having things too complicated. Three courses of something nicely served and tasty would have been very much more successful, and much easier for you, than six in a muddle – I'm sure you don't mind me saying this. I'm not critical, I simply want to help. Of course one of the snags in your job is that you're cooking for women, and often men as well, who are pretty good cooks themselves. Hallo, darling,' she added as Michael came in, looking him over with appraising eyes.

'How did you sleep?' he asked her.

'*Very* well. The kettle's broken.'

'That ass Simon.'

'Really? Then you must make him replace it. Quite honestly I do hate this attitude, that just because you're fairly well-off, other people can take advantage—' her voice trailed away down the hall as she accompanied him with a mug of coffee in one elegant hand and a piece of toast in the other.

Jess put on a clean skirt and top, scowling at herself in the glass, imagining how horrible she would look in white tailored trousers. It was true. Her figure was entirely feminine. When she went back to the kitchen, she found to her chagrin Michael at the stove, cooking bacon and eggs for himself. Roz was there too, pouring juice into two glasses.

'Sorry. I didn't know you wanted cooked.'

Roz said gently, 'You *could* lay the table.'

'In here?'

'Why not?'

Roz and Michael sat opposite each other. They didn't behave like lovers; they looked as if they had been married for rather a long time. Jess left them alone as soon as she could.

Christian did not appear.

Della said, 'Christian *here*? Are you *sure*? Where is he? Is he in the studio?'

'Yes.'

'But I haven't heard a *sound*!' For some reason this news was a shock. Della had been having what she called a relaxed morning, propped up in bed surrounded by the papers, the buzzer in easy reach. Now she was moving anxiously, as if she had to get dressed as quickly as possible. 'Why hasn't he been in to see me? Did he talk to you?'

'Not much.'

'I suppose he's run out of money. Does he look – rough?'

'A bit.'

'Well, run my bath, I'll get up at once. Does Michael know he's home?'

'He saw him, yes.'

'They don't get on. Still I can rely on Roz to keep the peace.'

She was reflecting on this, and Jess was in the bathroom when Roz looked in. 'Michael's very sweetly driving me to Dolchester to look for some shrubs for Mummy. We'll be out to lunch, will you tell Jessica?' She bent over Della and they kissed. 'Can we get you anything? Sure? See you later then. By-ee.' She closed the door gently, and Jess heard her happy feet skimming downstairs. But catching a glimpse of Della's face, she was shocked by the change in it. She looked like an old woman.

Her bathing costume had only arrived yesterday, though Josie vowed she'd posted it at once. Now with Michael and Roz out of the way, and Della dressing, she had an unexpected chance to swim. She pulled it on under her clothes, and ran out of the house and down to the pool. Although the sun had been up for hours, the grass was still dewy in the overgrown part of the garden, and her feet were soaked by the time she reached it. She stripped off her clothes and bundled up her hair in her cap, and then she ran along the top of the balustrade which divided the pool from the waterfall, and dived in. The coldness of the water took her breath with a delicious shock, before she struck out hard against the current and swam her fastest to the steps. Then she turned on to her back and let herself be carried most of the way, only twisting round at the last minute to use her strength against the flow. No matter how blue the sky was, the pool was always dark. She never tried its depth. She loved its mystery.

She played about for a while, until looking out of the water, she saw the boy Christian had joined her unseen and was sitting in the faded deckchair. She dived once more from the balustrade, but this time she swam underwater to the bank, and appearing almost at this feet, scrambled up onto the pavement beside him, ripping off her bathing cap and shaking out her hair.

'Do you always swim in that colour?'

'What's wrong with it?' She reached for her towel and began rubbing her neck and shoulders.

'Nothing. Like my sister – she always swam in black.'

'Aren't you going in?'

'No, I don't want to. Isn't it a bit dangerous, what you were doing? Diving like that?'

'There isn't that much of a current.'

'No, but if your foot slipped— You might fall the other way.'

'It's not that kind of stone. You've got a grip, even with wet feet.'

'Oh. Maybe you'll show me some time. I haven't swum here since— Not since Sylvie and I— We used to like it.'

She retired to put on her clothes. When she came out, he got up and they walked back to the house together. For lunch she made a Pavlova cake with the rest of the bananas and cream; he ate most of it. It was his idea to carry the food into the garden, and when Della joined them, very stiff and edgy, he arranged the long chair for her to recline in, and lay on the grass at her feet. Jess saw how she gradually dropped her guard, relaxed, until at the end of the meal, resting her hand lightly on his tawny, wavy hair, she exclaimed, it seemed without thinking, 'Oh Christian! you're so good – when you're good!'

'That's rather a double-edged compliment.'

But Della sighed, and lay back in the shade of the huge oak tree.

'Pass me the newspaper, darling, and help Jess clear away.'

'Can you spare her to tidy the stuido? he asked, plaintively. 'I do hate it to be in a mess, but I do hate putting things away.'

Della laughed. 'Well, if she doesn't mind, I don't need her.'

The studio had been made over the front rooms of the house, so that it was disproportionately long, with a low, steeply sloping ceiling. The walls were mostly covered with brilliant posters – travel scenes, pop groups, film stars – as well as black and white photographs of zoo animals blown up to monstrous size. There were scarlet rugs on the floor, and a peacock-coloured quilt on the divan; there was a screen with Chinese scenes painted on it by an amateur hand; the exercise bicycle was blue; the baby grand piano was black. Jess following Christian into this jumble of colours looked round, surprised. She thought it an oddly juvenile room for a married lady, as he said, 'This is all Sylvie's, I haven't added anything. It's just the way she had it.'

'Does anyone play the piano?'

'Not any more.' He flipped through the music lying on top of the piano. 'Do you?'

'A bit.' They were pop tunes simplified for beginners, hits from shows, all past history. 'These aren't difficult.'

She knew that he was looking at her, over the top of the piano. She began stacking the music, not making a very neat job of it. He said, 'You blush terribly easily.'

'I'm not. It's hot in here.' It was, so close under the roof, although all the windows were open.

'Oh, leave the music alone. All that about tidying was only an excuse to get you to myself. Come over here,' he said, moving to where the sun lit a golden square on the floor. 'Please come! I shan't hurt you.'

He sounded so ingenuous that she couldn't help smiling, and she went to stand beside him. 'Now I'm going to let you into a secret,' he said, very seriously. 'It's something Sylvie and I discovered; it's a short cut to knowing people – *I'm not joking!*' he added sharply, as her smile turned to a grin of embarrassment. 'It's a true way of finding things out, only you can only do it with special people. But obviously if you're going to shriek it won't work.'

'Sorry!' She was disconcerted. She didn't feel up to this test or game, particularly as hallowed by Sylvie. But she saw that he was determined to put her through it, though she couldn't help wanting to laugh.

'All you have to do is shut your eyes, and keep absolutely still. That's right.' The sun seemed to shine more warmly on her face when her eyes were closed. Presently she felt his fingertips, cool and light on her forehead. 'Don't flinch,' he said. 'I told you I wouldn't hurt you.' Gently, delicately, he moved his fingers to her temples, her cheekbones, the bridge of her nose. Suddenly she lost all desire to laugh. His almost stroking touch was hypnotic. He said, 'Did you realize that I've shut my eyes as well? You see I'm pretending to be blind.' He spoke in a monotone, so as not to interrupt the trance. 'I think you're rather easy to know. I thought you would be. You've got a jaw like a horse. When's your birthday?'

'Beginning of September.'

'Then you're a Virgo like me, but your lips aren't. They're fleshy. Don't you hate the word "flesh". It's an ugly, ugly word. I don't know about your eyes.' He moved his fingertips to her eyelids and kept them there for at least a minute. Then he said, 'I still don't know about your eyes. But I can feel them quivering under your skin. Like the wings of butterflies.'

Almost immediately he said, in a completely different tone, 'Do look! The tennis players!'

Michael and Roz had returned while they were

clearing away lunch. Now they came strolling round the house towards the court, dressed in white shirts, shorts and plimsolls, and carrying racquets and balls. 'A bit pompous, isn't it, for what's meant to be a game,' said Christian, his lips curled sardonically, and Jess, half-blinded by the sudden light, smiled too as she looked down on them. Michael went to the far end of the court and they began to knock up, elegant, accomplished. Sometimes they called to each other politely across the net.

'They make a good pair, don't they? Don't they?' he repeated more loudly, when she didn't answer.

'Yes.'

'She's determined to marry him. Don't you think so?'

'Probably.'

'Do you find him attractive?'

'If you like dark men.'

'Don't you?'

'I'm not bothered.'

'He's had lots of girls. Including my sister. Including my sister,' he repeated, so oddly that she looked quickly at him, but he had turned away and was wandering across the room, touching things, running his finger along the spines of a shelf of books, spinning the pedals of the exercise bicycle.

Jess began picking up the clothes that were lying heaped on the floor. He said at once, roughly, 'Leave them alone, will you? They belong to Sylvie.' So she drew back. But she couldn't help noticing how hard Sylvie had been on her clothes. They were all torn, at the hem, or under the arms – an expensive velvet jacket had the collar half ripped off. They wouldn't have fetched much on a stall, in spite of the fabrics.

Christian went over to the divan and lay down on it. 'You can play the piano if you want,' he suggested, wearily.

With Michael and Roz monopolizing the garden, she had nothing better to do. So she chose an album, sat down and started to play.

Between tunes she said, 'You're very like your mother.'

'That's a stupid thing to say!'

'Why? You both like being amused, and here I am doing it!'

He thought about this, and said, 'Anyway she's not my mother.'

Jess, her hands motionless on the keys, stared across at him.

'She adopted us. I'd have thought you'd have guessed that. You don't think we look like her, do you?'

'No, but that doesn't mean anything. I look like my father.'

'I don't know who ours was. I expect we were found under a gooseberry bush or something. She took us in because we matched the curtains. Go on playing. I didn't think I'd like it, but I do.'

After a while they heard voices just below, under the window. Jess looked at her watch. 'I must go. They'll be wanting tea.'

'No, stay where you are. Let them get their own.'

But she shut the lid, and stood up. He got off the divan. 'Will you be swimming later on this evening?'

It hadn't occurred to her. 'Why? Are you going to?'

'I might.'

'But I won't be free till after supper.'

'All right – what do you think – about nine?'

'Okay.'

They went downstairs together. Michael was coming up from the hall. The three of them met on the landing. He gave them a penetrating look, nodded without smiling, and went into his bedroom. Jess suspected that he was displeased, but after all it was none of his business what she did in her free time.

She looked foward to her evening swim. Christian was out for supper, but Della stayed up, and they had sandwiches with drinks on the terrace. Jess sat a little apart, on the steps. After the sun had gone down, its last invisible rays still caught the reds around them, when every other colour had died away. The old wall seemed to smoulder round the grey garden. But most of all, in the wooded slope across the river, the bell tower glowed as if it was on fire. It was always surprising to see it at sundown on a clear day, when at other times it was hardly distinguishable among the trees.

'Is there a bell any more?' asked Roz.

'Christian would know,' said Michael. 'He had a den in there when he was a boy.'

'He still is a boy, darling.'

'Hardly, He's nearly nineteen.'

'What's he going to *do*?'

'As a career, you mean? I've no idea. Has he spoken to you, Della?'

'He's still trying to make up his mind.'

Nobody, not even Roz, felt inclined to pursue the subject; perhaps they remembered that Jess was sitting there. A peaceful time, with the garden birds returning to their territories, cramming in their songs before dark.

Della's room was ready for the night. Jess had only

to clear the plates; then she hurried down to the pool. She avoided the terrace; they wouldn't have minded her swimming – why should they? – but still she went by a devious way. Christian wasn't there yet, but there was no point in waiting for him. In a few moments she was in the water, using her fastest stroke to keep warm. When she was out of breath, she hauled herself up by the balustrade and looked over. The view was misty and grey, and prickling with lights. The garden seemed somehow darker from the water – almost completely dark, in fact, and the little temple looked shadowy, romantic, where at any moment Christian should arrive.

It was nine o'clock – she heard the flat bell chiming in the church, at Palmers Cross presumably. She had just decided that he wouldn't come now, when she caught a movement between the bushes, and someone appeared strolling towards the temple. She recognized Michael at once, and he was closely followed by Roz. She didn't want to spy on them. As she poised to dive off the balustrade, she saw him stop dead, with the paleness that was his face turned in her direction. Then she cut the water, and did a fast crawl up the pool, expecting them to disappear if they wanted to be private. But as she surfaced, shaking the water out of her ears, she was amazed to hear Roz's voice, harsh and brittle with anger. 'Jessica! *What are you doing in there?*'

She looked round. Michael had gone. Roz was actually waving her arms in agitation.

'Come out *at once*! Do you hear?'

She turned and swam as close as she could to the place where she had left her towel and clothes; so that she was wrapped up by the time Roz reached her.

'Haven't you *any* idea? Didn't it cross your mind for one *second* that that's about the most *cruel* thing you could do in the circumstances? She was holding her voice low, which somehow added to its impact. She had stopped a little distance from Jess, as though she found her disgusting. Jess could only gape. 'You've just given him the most *appalling* fright. Do *stop* shaking your head and rubbing yourself! You've just behaved in the most *unfeeling* way. It was bad enough the way you were playing the piano this afternoon.'

Jess was making faces, she was upset, and kept rubbing automatically, and having to stop herself.

'I suppose if you thought at all, you thought he couldn't hear – when all the studio windows were open. I nearly came in and told you to stop it. I wish you'd seen his face. It's wicked – *wicked* of you, Jessica!'

'But I didn't know—'

'Now this!' Roz was goading herself, in case Jess was innocent. 'I thought he was going to faint.'

'But I can swim all right!'

'My *God*, It's nothing to do with that! Haven't you got *any* imagination? He thought you were a ghost – *her* ghost! *Don't you know? Sylvie was found dead in this pool.'* She looked at Jess and her anger changed to exasperation. 'I thought you knew. You were bound to know, from Mrs Drue or Christian or the village or anybody. Well, all right. Oh, don't start to *cry*! Get your clothes on and go back to the house. It's just bad luck it happened, that's all! Incidentally, have you got Christian's Walkman? He said he left it under the deckchair.'

'No,' sniff. Sniff. 'It's not here.'

'Bother. Michael gave it to him, and he must value

it, because he took the trouble to ring to ask him to bring it in, in case it got damp. Never mind. Do get a move on! I can hear your teeth chattering.'

Roz went. Left alone, Jess hustled on her clothes. Roz had been horrible, horrible – but it was far worse without her. Sylvie was all shapes in the shadowy temple. The black, smoothly moving water would never be empty again. It was full of Sylvie.

The bushes in this overgrown part of the garden looked like darkly cloaked figures. Jess ran between them with a beating heart.

Nine

After an hour or so, she couldn't bear it any longer. The house was dark. Barefooted, clutching her Indian wrap round her, she crept upstairs.

'I just wanted to say I'm sorry. I didn't know.'

He had thought, when he heard her discreet knock, that she was Roz. The last thing he wanted was psychoanalysis, or sex for that matter, and his expression, as he opened his bedroom door in pyjamas was fairly impatient. He was astonished to see Jess on the threshold. She interpreted his silence as anger.

'That's all. I didn't want you to think I did it on purpose.'

'That never occurred to me, as a matter of fact.'

Roz opened her bedroom door. 'I thought I heard voices.'

They looked at her without speaking.

'Goodnight, Michael,' she said chillingly, after a pause. She withdrew, and her door was gently, firmly shut.

'I'm sorry about the piano as well. I didn't mean to— to—'

'To what?'

Her lips trembled. 'To hurt your feelings.'

He said, in his slightly harsh way, I'm afraid you're the one that's been hurt.' She was silent. 'For your information I didn't love my wife – not by the time she died. It's just that your behaviour—'

'I'm sorry—'

'—your behaviour all round is a bit – unexpected.'

'I don't mean—'

'That's all right. I'm not complaining.'

She looked even younger than she was, he thought, her face pink with anxiety, her hair standing out like pale fire. But her body was a woman's. He suddenly wondered what she would do if he kissed her.

'You'd better go back to bed,' he said.

'Goodnight then.'

He switched on the light over the stairs, and waited until he heard the door close behind her. Then he went to bed himself.

Ten

Jess had dressed and laid the kitchen table, poured out the juice, made the coffee and cut the toast by the time Roz came down next morning.

'This is a little more civilized,' was all there was left to say, drily, as she took her place and unfolded her napkin.

'Did you sleep well?'

'Yes, thank you.'

'How much toast?'

'Two pieces, please. Oh, you've forgotten the marmite!' One to Roz. 'Don't worry. I'll get it.'

She spread a thin coating over her toast, while she considered how to tackle Jess on the delicate question of not going to Michael's bedroom in the middle of the night. Roz's mind was not quick. It worked easily on oiled tracks, but it had been put out of gear by her unexpected efficiency this early morning.

'Is this your first job away from home?'

'Yes.'

'You must find it quite tricky, having to live on the premises.'

'Not really. It's what I'm here for.'

'I don't think you quite get my point. It's a question of privacies. You have to learn when to be invisible. No, thanks, I'll have my coffee later, when Michael comes down. – It's lucky he's so long-suffering.'

Jess felt her cheeks burn. She kept her back to Roz, who went on, in her precise voice, 'Quite honestly he's amazingly patient with you, you know. He was perfectly beastly to the last girl. It was really a bit unfair. As I said to him, quite honestly you can't expect people from a different background to fit in straight away. I was completely straightforward about it, and I'm glad for your sake that he's turned over a new leaf.'

'What leaf?' asked Michael, coming in at that moment.

It was Roz's turn to blush. 'We were having a private conversation, and you've no right to creep in like that!'

'Do you want eggs and bacon?' Jess asked. Roz appeared astonished.

'Of course he does!'

He sat down at the table and said, 'I'll have to cry off Di's party. I'm going back to London this afternoon.'

'Oh, *Michael*. Why?'

'A stitch in time saves nine. I've got an appointment. Don't burn my bacon.'

'What on earth are you talking about?'

'The last bit was to the cook. – It's all right, you can drop me at the station, and go on to Di's with the car. Then you'll be free to come back tonight at your own speed. I can collect it from your place tomorrow, or the next day.'

'Your alternative engagement had better be something important. Poor old Di!'

'*She* won't mind. Two eggs, please, cooked both sides, I'm allergic to orange eyes in the morning.'

'You seem in very good form,' said Roz, resentfully.

'I am. Something to do with grasping the nettle. Great for morale, and the spirits generally.'

'Are you talking professionally?'

'Not necessarily.'

'Perhaps *Jess* knows what you're talking about,' Roz suggested after a pause. She couldn't keep the spite from her voice.

'Perhaps she does,' he agreed, laconically.

Jess put his plate in front of him, with the toast. Then she went out. Roz said, after a silence, 'Anyway you'd better impress on that one that girls who knock up men in the middle of the night are usually after one thing.'

'It depends on the girl,' he said. He was eating his breakfast with a good appetite.

'Not as far as you're concerned.' He said nothing. She went on, in a low, unusually passionate voice, so that knowing her as he did, he could tell how much it cost her to speak about it. 'I didn't mean to bring this up, but since we're on the subject, somebody told me they'd seen you with Lois.'

'What of it?'

'I thought you'd stopped seeing her.'

'Why should I? You're always saying we have a casual relationship.'

There was a pause, when he reached for more toast. His attitude spurred her to rashness. She said, 'Maybe I want to change that.'

'It's a bit late in the day, isn't it?' he said, looking her in the face.

He knew from the little pulse beating in the base of her throat how angry she was, but when she spoke her voice was light and controlled. 'I don't think I like you very much this morning. Quite honestly, you're impossible.'

He said, 'That's right and don't you forget it.' He got up and carried his empty plate to the sink. 'Coffee?' he asked, picking up the jug.

'Please.'

He filled their cups. He said, 'I thought Della could go with you this afternoon. And Jess. She hasn't had any time off. It'll do them both good to get out of the house.'

Roz was speechless for a minute. Then she said, sarcastically, 'You've forgotten Christian. And what about Mrs Drue? I'm sure Di would be thrilled to entertain them!'

'I've already arranged it,' he told her coldly. 'Of course if you want to drive back early, we can; we can drop them there first.'

'Obviously I have to go to Di's. I don't see why she should have her party blitzed at your convenience. She hasn't got a lot in common with Della – and damn all with Jess!'

Roz never swore. Michael grinned involuntarily, and quickly hid his mouth in his napkin. She finished her coffee, and left the room.

When Jess appeared to clear away, she found Michael still sitting at the table, and turned to go, but he called her back. She stood in front of him, unsure, picking at her fingers, exactly as if she'd been summoned by a school teacher. He said impatiently, 'Shut the door, will you? I don't want to be overheard.'

It was obvious that she thought she was in for a row. He softened his voice as much as he could.

'I've arranged for you to go out this afternoon, a friend is having people in, for swimming, and then there'll be wine and so on, I thought you'd enjoy it. You know her, she was here on Friday.'

'Thanks,' said Jess, in a guarded tone. 'I'd sooner stay here though.'

'No, I want you to go. You're employed to keep Della happy, and she's going. Roz will be there as well.'

'They won't want me along.'

'Rubbish, of course they will. Take your costume. You'll have a good time.' But she still looked obstinate, and wouldn't meet his eyes. 'You're going,' he said sharply. 'And that's it. Another thing, and this is much more important.' He looked at her, not altogether sure of how much to say. 'I suspect that it was Christian's idea, yesterday's late night swim? Or did you think of it?'

'He did.'

'That's what I thought. – Did he have his Walkman with him?'

'He never showed up.'

Michael got up and walked across to the sink, and stood with his hands in his pockets, looking out of the window. Presently he said, 'Do you like him?'

'Who? Christian?'

'Don't hedge.' He turned and observed her sternly.

'Yes, he's okay.'

'A nice, normal bloke like all the blokes you went to school with?'

'No, he's not like them,' she said at once

'Why not?'

'Well, because— because—'

'Go on because what?'

'He doesn't like the same things.'

'How do you mean?'

'Well he isn't into pop and sport and – all that.'

'What is he into?'

'I don't know— He's very— He talks a lot—' she glanced at him, embarrassed. 'He often mentions his sister.'

'You seem to have found out quite a lot about him already. Perhaps you ought to come with me to London.' And he actually seemed to be considering this, as she still stood in front of him, not at all understanding the purport of his interrogation. Then he startled her by asking abruptly, 'Has he kissed you?'

'No.'

But she blushed so much, that he couldn't be sure she was telling the truth.

'I'm not prying into your affairs.' He sounded exasperated. 'I'm not the least interested in who you kiss, or why. But I'd be easier in my mind if you'd keep him at arm's length. For the time being, I mean.' Pause. 'Do you understand?'

'Yes,' she said primly. She started to clear the table. He hesitated, wondering if he should have been more emphatic, but decided to drop the subject.

Di's house was the same sort as the Bell House – comfortable commuter country – but it was untidier and altogether more homely. There were weeds in the gravel and her dogs had scratched the front door. She looked nicer in a faded button-through red and yellow cotton dress and sandals, and seemed pleased to see them, Jess thought as she scrambled out of the back of Michael's two-door sports car. Della, slender and fragile in immaculate white linen with a white chiffon scarf round her head, and dark glasses, was escorted into the house and carefully settled near the picture window, so that she could see the swimming party without being exhausted by the sun. For this pool was close to the back of the house, and it was a comforting false blue surrounded by slabs of concrete, with a group of sunshine umbrellas at the far end where Di's friends had already gathered. Roz knew them all, and Jess was surprised and pleased to discover that she too recognized several people.

Bill came out with a jug of lemonade and plastic beakers. 'Aren't you the cook girl we met at Michael's?'

'Yes,' she said, shyly.

'Nice to see you. Come over and meet the folks.' He was naked except for bright boxer shorts. Most of his skin had been boiled red by the sun. He looked as though entertaining was a worry as well as a pleasure. He was not nearly so self-confident in his own place, without paper darts in his ears.

Roz and Di sat down together to chat. Jess helped to pass the drinks, and was hailed by a fat man with no chin, the colour of putty, who was sitting on the edge, dangling his feet into the deep end. When he took off his sunglasses, she saw that it was Sid Topper.

'Meet Chloe,' he said, and a tall girl with red hair and a green bikini helped herself to a mug of lemonade, and said, 'Hi.'

Dr Burgess and his wife were teaching their small children to swim at the shallow end. Jess watched them, the ideal family, cornflakes advertisement people; it must be good to belong to that sort of a group. Her own wouldn't fit in here. It wasn't only Doc that was wrong. Mum wouldn't be able to relax, and as for Josie, she wouldn't have the sense to keep her mouth shut.

'Are you going to take the plunge?' asked the girl called Chloe.

'Okay.'

The changing rooms were behind the umbrellas. Roz and Di were still engrossed in conversation; they had pulled their chairs away from the main group, but in here they could be heard clearly. They were discussing the oil business. Jess was ready in a minute, and running out into the sun, with the concrete warm underfoot, and the blue water sparkling enticingly, she suddenly dropped her inhibitions and bouncing as hard as she could on the safe little board overhanging the deep end, dived with a somersault into the water. There was a spontaneous cheer (even from Roz) as she came up, shaking her hair out of her eyes.

Chloe was good, too, but not quite as good as Jess.

'Doesn't your Dad keep a pub?' she asked later on, as they stood together waist-deep, getting their breath.

'Yes. How do you know?'

'Somebody told me— Mine used to have the Farmer's Arms, at Palmers Cross.'

'I thought he was a reporter.'

'My God!' exclaimed Chloe. 'Sid's not my dad; we live together. Why, does he look that old?' She stared across at him with dislike.

'He must be a good bit older than you.'

'That's why I won't marry him. He drinks like a fish as well. He told me he met you. He thought it was funny you going in there. That's where Sylvie Derby used to drink.'

Jess was shocked.

'Didn't you know? Drank herself to death, she did.'

'She didn't. She was drowned.'

'It's all the same thing. She stuffed herself with

whisky, and then she went swimming. They did a test. She was way over the limit.'

Chloe ducked and swam rapidly away underwater. Jess stayed where she was, overwhelmed by sickening thoughts. A minute later the red head bobbed up again beside her.

'It was Michael Derby's fault, anyway,' she remarked.

'How could it be? He can't have wanted her to drink.'

'Maybe not, but he wasn't very kind to her, was he?'

'How do you know?' Said Jess, with such passion that Chloe was surprised.

'Everyone knew! When she came up to the pub and started drinking, she talked all sorts about him. The whole village could hear.'

'That's not very pleasant!'

'They say she did it to get rid of the baby,' continued the relentless Chloe. 'Too bad she did herself in as well.'

'How horrible!'

Chloe looked at her curiously. She turned and flogged to the end of the pool, where she grabbed Sid's ankles and pulled him in. His sunglasses fell off but fortunately they floated and he was able to rescue them before she forced him to exert himself. Jess hauled herself out and padded along the side to the changing rooms.

'I hope Jess is enjoying herself,' said Di, noticing her overcast face. 'I thought she was getting on quite well with Chloe.'

'She's moody,' said Roz, with a glance.

Jess went into the changing room. She found her towel, and started to dry herself. Roz's voice sounded absolutely clear – even amplified by the wooden wall between.

'I must say I was a bit surprised to see Topper here.'

Di. 'You know what he's like – he asked himself. Don't tell me you care about *that* old history? I thought public opinion didn't bother you.'

'No, but it's lucky Michael's not here.'

'*Fisticuffs*, do you think? Oh, Topper can look after himself. You mustn't take Michael too seriously,' said Di. 'You know, I've always had a soft spot for him. I thought he was pretty sweet when he rushed out and rescued his cook person. Now come on, spill the beans. Has he actually popped the question?'

Jess, scarlet in the face, had just broken her bra strap. She wasn't neat-fingered at the best of times. She crouched, trying to make a knot that wouldn't burst under strain.

'Not in so many words,' Roz was saying, evasively. 'It's more of an understanding.'

'On his part as well?'

'Yes, of course! You've no idea how he takes me for granted. He'd be furious if *I* looked at anyone else!'

There was a marked silence. Jess's blood was pounding in her temples. Her fingers were all thumbs.

Di's voice. 'I think you ought to, if you want to bring him to the point. Old-fashioned, but it might work.'

'I'll remember, darling, thank you.' Roz sounded snappish.

Jess, hoisted into a lop-sided decency, crept out. The flower garden lay in front of her and she walked that way.

'I must do something about tea,' said Di. 'I thought I'd ask Jess to help me, where is she?'

'Not in the changing rooms listening to us, I hope, the little creep!' exclaimed Roz, twisitng round. 'No, it's all right, she's down there with her head in a rosebush.'

'You don't like her a bit, do you,' said Di, observing her with a barely concealed smile.

'No, I think she's lazy, and takes advantage. After last night, I don't even feel guilty about it.'

'You aren't just a tiny bit jealous?' Di suggested, wickedly.

'I shouldn't think so, quite honestly!' But Roz was stung, Di saw. 'How could I be?'

'Because she's *so* young, and thinks he's *so* fabulous. She has palpitations just being in the same room with him. Any man would fall for that, you know.'

There was a little arctic silence. Then Roz spoke. 'Perhaps your right, I ought to bring him on with somebody else.'

'I should,' said Di sweetly. 'It's time you took the initiative, after all you've been waiting three years.'

'You're a cat,' said Roz, with a wry smile.

'No, I'm not. But I do like him, and I think it would be a shame if he made any more – unsuitable alliances.'

Eleven

'I had a very pleasant afternoon,' said Della, taking off her scarf, and handing it to Jess to be folded and put away. 'Di is a very sweet person, even if her tea gives me indigestion. Perhaps you could mix me one of my powders. Dear me, how quiet the house is without guests. I quite expected Roz to stay to supper, but she doesn't really like driving Michael's car in the dark. It's a responsibility. Did you enjoy yourself?'

'Yes, thanks.'

'You seem a little *piano* this evening.' Della had taken on, in a quiet way, the further education of Jess, and when she looked up, surprised, explained, 'That, my dear, is Italian for low-spirited.'

'I'm a bit tired, that's all.'

'Then you must have an early night. An early night will do us both good.' She looked across at Jess, who was turning down her bed, and a thought crossed her mind – a shadowing thought. 'Is Christian about?' she asked, in a carefully nonchalant tone.

'I haven't seen him.'

'It's really time he learnt to organize himself. He's meant to go to college next term.'

'Where will he go?'

'Only to Dolchester. He has a room in a hostel there. He used to be at boarding school, but after— Well, that didn't work latterly, and he had to be removed. Not because he's stupid – oh, he's not stupid in the least. But he's not what I would consider—'

Jess waited.

'He's not entirely – stable.'

The room seemed to get darker in a bound.

'He was very close to his sister, and it's been hard for him.'

Della sat down, and thoughtfully removed her shoes. She stuffed the toes with balls of crumpled tissue paper, and Jess put them away in the wardrobe. She didn't expect to hear any more on the subject, but when she turned from the cupboard, she saw that Della was still sitting there, absorbed, and after a while she remarked, 'It's a pity really that he's so beautiful.'

She stood up with a sigh and began to undo the buttons of her linen dress. Jess helped her out of it, and held the silky housecoat for her to put on. Della said, not looking at her, 'I'm afraid any relationship with him would be unfortunate.'

'Do you want this washed?' Jess held up the linen.

'Only with the *greatest* care – on second thoughts, don't touch it. I'll set the machine myself in the morning. Fold it carefully into the basket – that's right. – What I feel I should perhaps make clear, my dear, is that I wouldn't want – I would be very *distressed* – if a girl I had become fond of – as it might be yourself Jessica – got involved with Christian.'

'That's okay,' said Jess embarrassed.

'Perhaps you think it's odd, me talking to you like this?'

'Mr Derby said something similar, earlier on.'

'Did he? That was thoughtful of him.' She turned to her chair, and sat down. 'I'm glad to hear that. When there are young people about— One feels responsible, and it's such a good idea, if one can, to avoid painful relationships.'

A discreet knock made them both jump, and they stared, very startled, at the door, which after a polite few seconds, opened. Christian stood there.

Della's colour had completely drained from her face, whose bones stood out as in death. Her hands gripped the arms of her chair, as if she would spring out of it, but she didn't move. Jess spoke to him, as roughly as she might have to Josie, 'Come down, you can give me a hand with supper.'

She thought he wouldn't follow her, but he did, noiselessly on his bare feet that were none too clean.

'What do you want to eat?'

'Nothing, Droobie gave me some supper. I only wanted to ask you something, but now you've been talked at by mother dear it's probably a waste of time.'

'She wasn't saying anything special.'

'I know what she said, I was listening.'

Jess began cutting thin slices of bread for Della's toast. He watched, and exclaimed, 'Either you've got to cut thicker, or sharpen the knife. Here, give it to me.'

There was a stone in the drawer. She watched as he honed the blade, expertly. 'Try that.'

It was like a razor.

'I used to collect knives. Sylvie and I had a brilliant game when we lived in London. We had a mean little garden with one of those paling fences, you know?' Jess nodded. 'Sylvie spreadeagled against it, and I threw knives round her outline. We got the idea from a circus. I never touched her.'

'Just as well,' said Jess, turning on the grill.

'She wasn't worried. She trusted me. It makes all the

difference, doesn't it, when somebody trusts you. – Look out, you're burning the toast. You aren't a very good cook, are you?'

'What was it you wanted to ask me?'

'If you'd come to a disco. There's one in the village at the weekend. I thought it might be nice to go.'

'What, me come and you won't be there?'

'Don't be like that! It wasn't my fault.'

She looked at him, and wondered how he had managed to survive, at all, the wreck of Sylvie's marriage. His expression sharpened.

'What's on your mind?'

'I don't go to discos with people that don't brush their hair or change their shirt or put shoes on their feet.'

'But I'll do all that,' he said at once. 'I'll dress up like a yob. I won't say I'll come here to pick you up – is Michael back next weekend? But if you start walking up to the village on the Saturday night, I'll jump out of the hedge, that thin bit just past the postbox—'

'With straw in your hair.'

'No, really not! And we'll have a good time.'

'Maybe.' She was arranging Della's tray. 'Remind me about it on Friday.'

'Okay, or if I can't get to the house, I'll send you a card or something. I've got to be in Dolchester this week, sorting out this college business. Do you want me to carry up that tray?'

'It's okay, thanks.'

'I like the flower by the plate, it's little touches like that dear Mummy appreciates. By the way I've been thinking a lot about you, and I can't make up my mind whether you're exceedingly cunning, or amazingly simple. We'll have to play fingers again.'

'Not now,' said Jess with the tray, trying to pass him in the doorway.

'No, not now. In a quiet moment.'

When she came down again, he had gone.

Twelve

Later that week, two cards came for Jess. One was from Rachel, a black and white view of Crouch End. Her job teaching English to the five children of an Italian count had fallen through and she was working in the salon. At the bottom she had written I loathe it, or I love it, in such a scrawl that Jess couldn't make out which, but guessed loathe. The other was from Doc, a picture of a barefoot boy in dungarees giving a bunch of flowers to a maiden in a long frock and bonnet. LOVE TO MY GIRL X SEE YOU was printed on the back, and it had taken a long time in the post, but even so, when the bell rang early next morning and she opened the front door, she was utterly astonished by her visitors.

She stood on the threshold, thunderstruck, speechless with her mouth open, her hand still on the white painted edge of the door as if she might shut it in their faces. Poor old Doc was looking unsure in the mushroom sports shirt, his best, and cotton trousers belted into the crease between his hips and his stomach, so that they dragged at the heels. Josie – how would Della bear her? – looked pert as ever in her tightest jeans with white socks and high heels, and the dreadful sleeveless black T-shirt with the buttons ready to pop off down the front. And it was so nice of them to come – they must have left at first light, to turn up before Mrs Drue; but only just, because here she was arriving. So Jess croaked, 'Hi! What a surprise!' and motioned them in before Doc could treat the daily help to an exhibition of a father/daughter embrace.

'Mum got your card,' he said, as if it was an explanation, after he had kissed his eldest in the comparative privacy of the kitchen. 'We came as soon as we could.'

'What card?' Jess was completely bewildered. She put the kettle on. Mrs Drue came in. 'Visitors?' she beamed at Jess. She mouthed the word 'Hallo!' at Josie, said to Doc, 'I've just tucked my tiny car in behind yours, not touching,' and removing her plastic container of polishing things from the cupboard, glided smilingly away.

'Is that the invalid lady?' asked Doc, in a low voice.

'Of course not! That's the daily. D'you want coffee, or tea?'

'Aren't you glad to see us?' asked Josie resentfully.

'Yes, but I wish I'd known you were coming.'

'What's this for?'

'*Don't touch it*! It's for the waste. Here, sit down,' she almost pushed them on to stools. The buzzer gave them all a jump. 'I've got to go. I won't be long. Here, Josie, make the instant.' She fled.

Della was standing by the window in her dressing gown, looking down on the rusty Peugeot estate that was the family car. 'Visitors! At this hour.'

'It's Dad and my sister.'

'Oh. I didn't know they were coming.'

'Nor did I.'

'They've taken Mrs Drue's space, she always parks by the staddle stones.'

'She doesn't mind.'

'All the same it might be better if they moved. It is her usual place.'

'Okay. I'll go and tell him.'

Doc shifted the Peugeot, with much revving and sputtering of gravel on to the lawn and flowerbeds. Jess was conscious of Della's critical eye upon him. Presently she buzzed again.

'I think, as your family have come all this way to visit you, you ought to have the day off.'

'No, really, it's okay,' said poor Jess, crimson with embarrassment. 'I can manage. They can sit in the kitchen with me, they won't mind.'

'No, my dear, that wouldn't be right, you must take the day and enjoy yourselves. How long are they staying?'

'Only till after lunch, I should think; Dad'll have to be back for opening— opening—'

'Opening what?'

'Opening the house for Mum, she couldn't come with them, she's working today.'

'They say you can get quite a reasonable lunch at the King's Arms in Dolchester if your father doesn't mind a pub. I believe the new manager's quite a pleasant sort of man. Now I shall get dressed, I look forward to meeting them before you all go out. No, my dear, it's not the least trouble. A little treat will do you good.'

Josie had produced a brightly coloured beach bag. 'I brought my suit,' she announced. 'I want to swim.'

'You can't.'

'Why not? You do.'

'What Mum wants to know,' Doc said heavily, spooning sugar into his mug, stirring it round and round until Jess could have shrieked with irritation, 'is how soon you've got to leave; for that matter you can come back with us if you like.'

'If I got the push I wouldn't want to work in the place another minute. I'd walk straight out,' Josie stuck her oar in.

'I haven't got the push.'

'You told Mum you had!'

'I said *probably*!'

'It's the same thing.'

'It's not.'

'It would be for me!'

'It isn't with me, and I'm staying.'

'Girls,' said Doc. He looked up under his eyebrows as Mrs Drue came in again, threading her way through the unusually crowded kitchen with smiling goodwill.

'That woman gives me the pip,' said Josie.

'Keep your voice down!'

'What for! She thinks we're scum, you can tell at a glance.'

Mrs Drue came back with the mop, her seer's eyes meaningly fixed on the middle distance. She closed the door behind her with expressive softness.

'I'm bored,' said Josie. 'Show me the other rooms. I want to see your bedroom.'

'Come on then.'

Josie bounced on the bed and tried all the taps, but Doc wouldn't cross the threshold. 'This is very fine,' was all he said.

Josie and Della met on the stairs. Della was taken aback; she cleared her throat. 'You must be Jess's sister.'

'Pleased to meet you,' said Josie.

'And I you,' she returned politely. She came down

into the hall and shook hands with Doc. 'What a beautiful day! Do you know, I don't think we've had a drop of rain since Jessica's been with us.'

'I'm glad she's making herself useful,' he mumbled.

'Please can I swim? I brought my things,' said Josie at her elbow.

'Oh – but we don't swim here,' Said Della at once.

'Jess does.'

Della looked at Jess and then her face cleared, and she said brightly. 'That was in someone else's pool. I'm afraid it's not possible today. But Jess will show you the garden.'

The three of them went outside. Jess showed off the tennis court.

'We could have a game,' suggested Josie.

'We don't play properly.'

'So what? We could muck about,'

'It's not that sort of place,' It was oddly hard to explain, when her view of it would never be Josie's. 'They do things in style. Even when they're mucking about like you said, they put on white clothes.'

Della was sitting in the drawing-room with the paper, but Jess knew she was keeping an eye on them. Doc was ill at ease. He said, 'That's fine,' when he looked at things, or drew in his breath admiringly.

They stared at the river, but Josie wasn't interested in following it down the garden, and Jess didn't lead the way. Doc said, 'I've got a feeling I ought to get that car off the driveway.'

So they collected the beach bag, said goodbye to Della and drove to Dolchester to pass the time before lunch. Doc bought some plants to fill in gaps in the window boxes at the White Posts. He was clearly relieved to be away from the Bell House, but Josie was inclined to grouse.

'If you'd said what it was like I wouldn't have bothered to come,' she told Jess, when they were in the Ladies' at the King's Arms.

Doc was having a conversation with the girl behind the bar, who happened to be Chloe. They had sandwiches and cider, and Doc had beer. He pretended it tasted quite different from beer in London. He peered into the paper bag containing his little pots of plants, and remarked, 'You can tell these flowers were grown in the country.'

As he was paying, Chloe looked at Jess over the top of the till and said, 'There's a disco Saturday night at Palmers Cross. Fancy going?'

'I might. How about you?'

'I could do with time off Sid. I can't get there much before nine though. See you then.'

'Okay. See you.'

The glamour of the Bell House seemed to have rubbed of on Jess, from Doc's point of view. He listened respectfully when she said anything, but seemed to find it easier to talk to Josie. It made Jess feel lonely. She wrote her mother a card while they were having their sandwiches. Later, she stood in the lane outside the Bell House, and waved until the old car had bundled out of sight. She was glad when they went; that was the truth, and it was no good feeling guilty about it.

Thirteen

All that week Christian stayed away, and he didn't ring or write, so there seemed no reason to mention him in connection with the disco, when she told Michael about it. She said she was going with Chloe.

'Sid Topper's girlfriend? Tall, with red hair?'

'That's right.'

'She's a barmaid.'

'So am I.'

'It's a type, Jessica, not an occupation. How are you getting there?'

'I'll walk up. She'll drop me home, she's got the use of the car.'

He said no more about it, but she knew that he disapproved. It was certainly easier to discuss it on the phone than it would have been face to face, when she could see how quickly she exasperated him. She didn't know how this would ever change.

Della said, 'That was the rather elegant girl in green at the swimming party? I forget what she was called.'

'Chloe.'

'Such a pretty name. I daresay you'll enjoy it. All those coloured lights. Won't the music be rather loud?'

'It always is.'

'Do you like to dance?'

'Yes, I love it.'

'So did I, but of course in my day it was a very different thing. Men had respect. That's all gone today, I'm afraid.'

Jess reflected, as she drew the curtains, that whenever Della had been born she would have been old-fashioned.

She meant to put on her blue dress for the disco, the one she'd last worn for the dinner party, but when she took it out of the cupboard she found a gaping hole between the sleeve and the bodice. She must have ripped it when she took it off, and she certainly hadn't time to mend it now. Instead she squeezed herself into a tight black skirt with a slit that Josie had encouraged her to buy, and the white broderie anglaise top that she'd worn – how long ago it seemed – for her interview. She made up her face with care, and tied the scarf Della had given her round her hair.

'Is this my hot drink for later?' asked Della, seeing the thermos on the tray. 'You're very thoughtful, my dear. Well I hope you have a nice evening. Have you got the key? And you'll lock up before you go. Don't be *too* late. I wonder if you could make me one more piece of toast. Only if you have time. Thank you so much.'

And when she brought it, '*Could* you run down and get me the little wireless? So stupid of me – I left it in the drawing-room, or if it isn't there, perhaps it's in the hall.'

So that one way or another, she was late in starting, and the tight skirt made it difficult to hurry. She concertinaed it well above the knees and scuttled along as quickly as she could. She didn't expect Christian to jump through the hedge, and he didn't; but she did miss Rache. She could have done with a bag of curried crisps and some lighthearted chat.

She could hear the thump of the music as she came up the hill into the village. The disco was in the old school, and the playground, and the square by the church were full of bikes and cars. As she approached, she recognized a Beatles tune. Several boys were hanging round the entrance, joking and drinking out of cans, but she avoided their eyes as if she'd already got a partner waiting for her inside, and bought her ticket. Drinks were on sale, beer and cider, and glasses of squash. She asked for a lemon, and took it to the room where people were dancing, and stood just inside the door. The disc jockey was very tall and thin, and called himself Wee MacGregor. He wore a kilt and a tam o'shanter, and talked with a mock Scottish accent. Soon her eyes adjusted to the darkness and the coloured shapes flicking round the ceiling, and she spotted Chloe snaking by herself in a corner, so she edged round in that direction.

Chloe was wearing a strapless green top with black velvet trousers and high heels. Several boys were watching her, but for the moment she took no notice of them, she seemed pleased to see Jess however. They danced side by side for a while. In spite of its lofty ceiling, the room was fearfully hot, as well as noisy. It seemed impossible that any more people could fit in, and yet they appeared, and were absorbed. The boys seemed inclined to pester Chloe, without bothering much about Jess. She was used to this; Rache always got most of the passes. Chloe said, 'God I'm sweating, shall we go and get ourselves a drink?' and she forged through the dancers with Jess and the most persistent of the fans following.

'Have a beer,' she said when they finally made it to the bar.

'Cider, please.'

The drinks were warm, but good. Jess bought the next round. Then one of the admirers offered to treat them, which gave Chloe a chance to be surprised by his existence, and imitate his accent. This struck Jess as funny, and when Chloe started to talk about Sid, about how he would be sitting in front of the television drinking Scotch and scratching himself in the armpits, in his socks that had a built-in deodorant, she went on laughing. She really liked Chloe and she followed her dizzily into the Ladies' Toilet and then they had another beer and another cider, and as they were jigging back for more dancing her shoe came off, which was pretty funny as well, and didn't matter because she danced better in bare feet. She liked the Beach Boys just as much as the Beatles. She was really enjoying herself, when a grey-haired man (her usual luck) with hot eyes and bad breath turned up. He seemed to think he belonged to her, and he was becoming increasingly difficult to ignore, while Chloe was having problems as well. Things were getting confused when somebody pulled down the drapes covering one of the tall windows, and they were all suddenly submerged under black material, and there was a lot of screaming and thumping before it was sorted out.

That let the moon in. And even though they managed to hoist the drapes halfway with the long pole used for opening and shutting the top windows, her disco mood might have started to disintegrate, except that Chloe and some of the boys had a cache of beer in their corner. Beer was better than nothing when you were thirsty, but she wasn't going to share a can with the old man all the same, and she wasn't going to sit on his knee either. She was very glad when the cold finger of the moon rested on Christian across the room, and she waved with both arms and put them round his neck when he was close enough. His white shirt was open to the waist and he was the most beautiful man she'd ever seen. She danced in front of him, singing little bits of the tunes booming round the wall, but all the time a clear fraction of her brain wondered whether he was stoned. He danced – if you could call it dancing – as if he was sleep-walking. Moon-struck, he looked.

The church clock struck eleven. The old man had gone, and Chloe was what Mum would call up to all sorts in the corner where the beer cans, empty and full, were rolling under the chairs. Jess tried to say to Christian, 'It's good you came,' but her tongue felt too large for her mouth, and prevented her voice from sounding like her own when she managed to get it out. And still that clear particle of her brain, observing him, noted that his face looked odd – as if the halves of it had slipped, and come together out of line.

Wee MacGregor was clicking his fingers to the rhythm, while he kept a watchful eye on the scene. Christian put his hands on Jess's waist. They didn't feel like a dancing partner's hands. They were cool, and constrictive. She wriggled a bit, to show she didn't like it, but he held her more tightly. His lips were set in a little, humourless smile.

'Why do people come to this sort of thing?' he asked her, keeping his voice low.

'It's fun, isn't it?'

'Is it?'

As they twisted to and fro in the crowded room, she wondered whether he had ever been to a disco before. He was absolutely not part of the scene. And between his hands she was becoming increasingly isolated from the other dancers; and by and by she began to feel, for some indefinable reason, menaced.

She said, 'You don't have to stay if you aren't enjoying yourself.'

'That's all right. I'll walk you home.'

'No, I've got a lift. I'm not walking.'

He didn't answer, but as they turned again in the dance, Jess glanced at Chloe and felt a twist of panic.

He moved closer and said softly, 'We could leave now.'

'No,' I'll wait for the end.'

'We could go outside for a bit.'

'No, thanks.'

Fright was chilling her alcoholic glow. She didn't like being held as close as this, feeling his hard body through her clothes. Apart from anything else, it made him impossible to dance with, for he was oddly unmusical, almost out of step with the rhythm.

'Are you enjoying yourself?' he asked her in a low voice.

'Not a lot.'

'Why not? Aren't I doing it right?'

She hiccoughed and said, 'I'm afraid you'll tread on my feet. I'm not wearing shoes.'

He said nothing to this, and they blundered on.

She said,'Okay, well I'd better find the girl who's driving me back.' She wanted her voice to sound loud and confident, but she couldn't control it properly. When she tried to break away, he moved one of his hands from her waist to the back of her neck.

'Stop that,' she said. 'Get off.' But she wished she hadn't drunk so much. Her body wouldn't do what she meant it to. She raised her voice. 'Let go of me, will you?' People looked round, deflecting him for a moment so that she managed to wrench free. He caught up with her in the doorway. 'I'm going to the toilet,' she said, loudly.

She didn't glance at the mirror as she passed it. She felt a wreck. But the window only opened six inches. She was considering locking herself into one of the compartments for the night, when a drab elderly woman entered and looking at her as if she was something the cat brought in, said, 'Hurry up, dear, people are waiting outside.'

Including Christian. She pushed past him and went back to the dance floor, desperately scanning the crowd for red-haired Chloe who seemed to have disappeared. She felt his hand on her shoulder, his arm encircled her waist like a steel spring; they were dancing again, as close as ever. It was almost twelve, the dance would finish, and Chloe was nowhere to be seen. Clamped to Christian, Jess stared to cry, invisibly in the darkness, without sobs.

Suddenly, he stopped dead. She twisted round, and saw with a shock Michael Derby standing beside them. He said to her, 'What are you doing here?'

Christian said, 'If I ask my girl to a party and she accepts, it's none of your bloody business.' His voice sounded thick and strange.

Michael spoke only to her. 'Get your things. I'll take you home.'

For a minute Jess thought Christian would strike him, and perhaps he did too; he waited, tall and still. Then Christian said, 'You bastard,' in the same odd voice, and walked out, very straight, without a backward glance. Jess poked about in the dark under the chairs and found her bag.

'What have you done with your shoes?'

She remembered kicking them under the table in the bar. As she grovelled, she felt her skirt split another seam. Everything looked indescribably squalid. Her face was flaming.

They went out into the night. The shadow of the church was huge across the grass. As they crossed the road, the clock struck twelve. Her head was reeling in the fresh air, and she had a horrible feeling that she was going to be sick. His car was close and he opened the passenger door. 'Sit in the front,' he said curtly, as she was about to scramble through behind the seat. 'There's not much of that skirt left. I'm trying to get you back in one piece.'

He got in beside her.

'You said you were going with Chloe,' he said, after a silence.

'I did. I didn't think Christian would come.'

'But he asked you.'

'Yes.'

'And you accepted.'

'More or less. Yes.'

Her head was throbbing as if it would burst. All round them, engines were revving, cars and bikes were pulling away. He started up, and they drove off. No more was said until he stopped in front of the Bell House. There was the faintest glow from Della's window, that was her nightlight; otherwise, all was dark. Jess tried to get out quickly, but muddled the handles and locked herself in instead. As he reached past her to open the door, he suddenly turned his face and kissed her on the lips. He took her completely by surprise, and he too was surprised, because she felt like a child – that was the only way he could describe it to himself. And she wasn't one. That pub with the father and mother and sister flashed through his mind. So he kissed her again, and this time she tried to avoid him, but he held her in place until he had finished. Then he looked at her, and said at once, 'Why are you crying?'

'I'm not.' Tears were streaming down her face.

'Have you got a headache?'

'Splitting.'

'I'll find you some painkillers.'

'It's okay, I've got some.'

He moved away and she opened the door and got out. He unlocked the house and followed her in. The moon shone into the hall and they didn't need the light. She walked ahead of him to her room, went in and closed the door. He locked up and went to bed.

She ripped off the little black skirt and rolled it into a ball, and shoved it into the wastebin. Then she took off the rest of her clothes and had a shower. By the time she brushed her hair she had stopped crying, but still she couldn't meet her own eyes in the glass. She got into bed. Her head ached with a sickly black pain and she didn't think she would sleep, but in fact she soon drifted into a doze.

Only minutes seemed to have passed when she jerked awake again, with the idea that somebody had tapped on her door. Her head felt better. She lay tense, listening, her heart beating quick and hard.

It came again, the lightest of knocks. A low voice said, 'Jess.'

It was Michael. She switched on her bedside lamp, and got hastily out of bed. She said against the door. 'What do you want?'

'Let me in quickly. I need your help.'

It didn't occur to her to ask questions. She opened her door.

He was deathly pale, almost as white as the sheet which he had wrapped round himself and clutched with his right hand to his left shoulder. He came in and she shut the door quickly. He was swaying where he stood. He said faintly, 'I'm afraid there's blood, don't scream, we can do without Della.' But she was staring with horrified eyes at the redness spreading between his fingers. She pulled back the quilt and steadied him on to her bed. His blood was spreading, spreading, and for a few moments she herself felt horribly faint. She pulled herself together and went into the bathroom. She soaked the cleanest of her towels in cold water, wrung it out and folded it into a pad, then gently drew back the sheet. The wound with the blood coming out was enough to turn her stomach. He twisted his head on the pillow as she laid on the pad, but made no complaint. She moved quickly to the door. He mumbled, 'Where are you going?'

'To call the doctor.'

'No!' To her horror, he struggled to sit; he said, 'Don't go out there.' He gasped for breath, and said, 'Bolt the door.'

She did this. A crimson tinge was colouring the towel. He said, 'Christian. He may be in the house.'

He fell back and shut his eyes. Perhaps he fainted; she couldn't tell. She prepared another cold water compress, and put it to the wound. There were red spots on the fitted carpet. At the third change, she could see that the blood flow was less. At that point it occurred to her to lock the French window, and the small one into the bathroom.

He opened his eyes. 'Sticky stuff, blood,' he murmured.

She rinsed out her face flannel and washed his hands. She rinsed it again, and sprinkled cologne on it, and wiped his face. His nose was sharp under the cloth.

'That's nice,' he said more clearly.

'Are you warm enough?' she had covered most of him with her quilt.

'Yes. It's surprisingly pleasant lying here. Your peacefulness must have got into the bed.'

Later he asked for a glass of water. She supported his head with one hand, and held it to his lips. He smiled and said, 'Don't look so anxious. It's only a flesh wound.'

After the drink, he went to sleep for a little. She went on changing the towels, and between times sat by the bed. The clock in the hall struck three, but when she peered between the curtains, the night seemed as dark as ever. Soon after this, she heard stealthy footsteps in the passage. They tiptoed up to her door; presently the handle was gently turned. Jess sat transfixed with her eyes staring and her heart hammering. The handle was turned again – rattled. Michael stirred, and muttered, but didn't wake.

Somebody laughed loudly just outside the door. It must have been Christian, but it didn't sound like him. He rapped several times, very sharply and quickly, on the wooden panels of the door. Michael opened his eyes and looked at Jess. He reached for her hand. She gripped his, tightly, until at last the laughter and the knocking stopped, and the steps crept away.

'What about Della?' Jess whispered, hollow-eyed.

'Nothing. He won't touch her. He can't, I locked her in as I passed.'

Sleep had done him good. He was a better colour, and the wound had stopped bleeding. He said, 'I was coming out of the shower, and there he was in the open window. He aimed for my heart. I was lucky.'

He had another drink, and went back to sleep. Jess sat looking at him, without noticing the time. There would be no letter, no photographs. She wanted his face indelibly on her heart.

At last, when the night began to ebb, the dead dawn colour to streak the sky, she was overcome by tiredness and dropped asleep in her chair. When she woke, very late, her bed was empty, and the quilt had been tucked round her with a careful hand. The bloodstained sheets and towels were tumbled on the floor. She washed and dressed quickly, and left her room. The front door was wide open and sunlight was streaming into the hall. Dr Burgess' car was parked in the drive. She heard voices upstairs, and Michael met her on the landing. He too was dressed, and though pale, appeared much as usual.

'Just in time,' he said in his dictatorial way. 'You can pack for Della.'

She was sitting on the side of the bed. Behind her, Dr Burgess was cheerily fastening his bag.

'She's off for a spot of hight living,' he announced for Jess's benefit. 'A few weeks' spoiling by trained medical staff will do her the world of good. He patted Della on the shoulder as he whisked past. 'She'll come back a new woman!'

Della said nothing; her hands were clenched in her lap; her eyes were fixed, as though on some fearful apparition only visible to herself.

The doctor lingered on the landing, talking to Michael.

'Don't be a fool, you know quite well you oughtn't to drive. Put her on a train, or get one of your girlfriends to do it – ask Roz, she's over at her mother's, she'd be glad to help.'

Jess assumed that they were talking about Della, but later on that morning, streamlined transport arrived for her with the name of a nursing home in unobtrusive lettering.

During the packing, Della was unnaturally silent. 'Have you put in my sewing things?' she asked, several times, as though they were some sort of talisman, or link with rational life, that she could work at in order to return to normal. And once she said, out of the blue, 'If he's damaged any of your clothes, you must tell Michael. Don't forget. Anything damaged will be replaced.'

'Okay, thanks.' Jess was rolling up stockings. Della never wore tights.

'It will weigh on my mind, if he's spoilt anything of yours. I don't know how far he went with his devilment.'

Jess remembered then the rip in her best dress; and Sylvie's clothes, all torn one way or another; and the silk shirt Della was making for Michael. The thought of Christian working through their belongings was not pleasant.

She carried the suitcases down to the hall, where they were removed by a perfectly groomed young woman in uniform. Della came downstairs very slowly, with her mouth half open as if she was trying to scream. Michael was beside her. Jess and the nurse waited at the bottom. In the doorway, Della turned to Jess and unexpectedly put her arms round her, and kissed her.

The chauffeur opened the door of the car, and Michael helped her inside. The nurse sat beside her in the back. So without a wave, or even a glance from her haunted eyes, Della was driven smoothly away.

Michael and Jess went back into the house. He said, 'I'm going to crash out for an hour. Make something to eat, will you? No rush. I'll come down when you're ready.'

She went into the kitchen, and waited until she heard him shut his bedroom door. Then she wrote on a piece of paper, 'I'm sorry but I can't stay. I hope Mrs Fry will be better soon. Take care JX.' She put it under the salt cellar in the middle of the table, and then she went into her room and pushed all her things into her suitcase. She was ready to go in ten minutes. She looked once round the room where so much had happened, and a rush of tears came to her eyes. Then she left, closing the front door quietly behind her, walking quickly down the drive. All the way to the village, she had a wild idea that he might come after her; whenever she heard a car, she longed for it to be his. Some of the time she cried. She couldn't seem to stop the water coming out of her eyes.

The barman at the Farmer's Arms called her a taxi, and she waited a miserable twenty minutes for it, without the heart even to eat a sandwich. Everything was folding up behind her; soon she would be back at the White Posts as if none of it had happened. She caught the afternoon train from Dolchester with ten minutes to spare. Michael just missed it. He sat fuming in the station car park, with her note crumpled in his hand, and a savage pain in his shoulder.

Fourteen

'Mrs Fry got worse, that's all. She had to go to a clinic.'

'You're upset, Pet. What's upsetting you?'

Mum's arm round her shoulders made her cry all over again. 'I'm fond of her. You get fond of people when you look after them.'

'She's not that ill, is she? Maybe she'll want you back.'

'No.'

Michael gave her an hour to cross London, an hour to settle in. Then he rang. He was furious.

'I thought I asked you to cook me a meal.'

'I'm sorry. I didn't have time.'

'What the hell made you rush off like that? What sort of monster do you think I am? I had every intention of driving you home.'

'You couldn't, not with your shoulder.'

'Rubbish, the car's automatic, and perfectly comfortable. It's not as if it was a jeep. Anyway, how much good do you think it did me, tearing round the countryside after you on an empty stomach?' Silence hissed between them. 'You realize I'm not obliged to pay you notice when you walk out like that?'

'I don't want money.'

'Oh, be your age.' Another hissing pause. 'Has Christian got your address?'

'No.'

'All right. That's something, at any rate.'

There was a question she had to ask. 'What are you going to do about him?'

'Live here at weekends until he shows up again. He'll be back.'

'But the police—' she suggested, anxiously.

'He's not a police case.'

'But you mean – Like bait—'

'That's about it.'

She didn't know what to say then, and he hung up.

'She's lost pounds,' said Judy to Doc in bed that night.

'What can you expect? I was against it from the first. A flash in the pan, that's what I thought. All the same,' he said, remembering, staring up at the ceiling, 'it was lovely place. Carpets, pictures. Tennis courts.

Jess was dreamy, worse than usual. She cried easily. Josie was shriller than ever. The dead freesias were still in their vase between the beds. Jess wrapped them in tissue paper and hid them in the drawer under her clothes.

The pain of missing him didn't get better as the weeks passed. She suffered too because it was impossible not to compare being at home with her life at the Bell House. She felt greedy, disloyal – but in fact it was the discipline she missed. Under Della she had accepted this as a moral benefit, without even realizing it. At home, any discipline was reduced to producing good value for money in the shortest possible time, and she found she became exhausted, far more quickly than before, and felt she had been beaten round the head. Worst of all, she saw that her parents were sorry for her, and wished things could be different. They would have settled for more money, but Jess was perceptive enough to know that that was only the surface of the problem.

'It's a mistake, letting them into a different environment. Gives them ideas,' said Doc in the bar.

'She hasn't been right since she got back,' Judy complained to Rachel's mother, on her monthly visit for a rinse and shape.

'Oh, they're a worry girls,' said the hairdresser, who never worried about anything.

It was true that Jess was still losing weight, and she was pale, with rings under her eyes.

A pale green envelope came for her in the post, addressed in a dark green, flowing hand, and forwarded from the Bell House. It was from Chloe.

'Hi! Thought I must write and tell you the news of the year – I've joined the Pudding Club – Sid is thrilled and were getting married – surprise surprise yes no?' She skimmed down the page with a beating heart – 'Mrs Frys still in the bin, M Derby comes back a lot, they say hes always alone and him such a ladies man proberly going round the bend as well – that Christian you liked hasnt been seen since the night of that disco when we got pissed but it was good fun wasnt it – wish we'd had more time to do things – Let me know if your back in the area – you can always get me at the Kings Arms or through Dad at the Feathers—'

This letter unsettled Jess. It suggested a scene which her imagination caught and painted with dramatic detail – the spectral house at night; the figure flitting from bush to bush in the darkness; Michael alone, asleep upstairs; Christian at his window with the knife he had honed to a lethal sharpness. She lay in her old narrow bed and pictures filled her mind until her nightdress was soaked with sweat. She saw the bulge behind the curtain, the bare feet noiseless on the carpet. Michael moved in his sleep and Christian retreated, but he was still there, and he would go on being there, until his chance came.

Jess couldn't listen to the outrages in the paper which Josie liked to read aloud with squeals of horror. Her waking nightmares about the Bell House were getting worse, beginning to colour her life like a spreading stain. She would stand in a daze at the table or the sink, with her heart throbbing painfully for no reason. She would go to the shops, and come back with the wrong things. Her mother would have given a lot to know what was the matter with her, but nobody had ever listened much to Jess, and she wasn't going to talk now.

One evening, nearly a month after her departure from the Bell House, she was carrying a plate of sandwiches through to the bar. She was walking down the dark little passage where the telephone was, when she heard his voice. 'Jess,' he said, and again, 'Jess.'

She started violently, and looked round. He sounded so close, so clear, that she didn't doubt he was standing behind her. The shock made her gasp, set the blood burning in her face.

But he wasn't in the bar, or in the kitchen. It was a Friday night, and they'd been in a rush all day. She went upstairs early, pretending she had a headache. She went into her parents' room where the safe was; Doc visited the bank on Fridays but even so she knew it would be full of money. She scooped out all the notes and fastened the safe, and went on into her bedroom. She was just putting on her coat when she heard feet on the stairs. Josie.

'What have you got your coat on for?'

'I'm cold. *Leave that*! Just too late she made a grab, but Josie's sharp eyes had already spotted the heap of money on the bed.

'Are you in a gang?' Josie's voice was hushed with awe.

'No!' She started pushing the notes into her bag. 'Don't worry. I'll pay it back.'

'Are you running away from home?'

'No.'

'You might tell me. I won't talk!'

And she'd have to, because a shout from Josie would bring Mum running.

'Are you going Back to Him?'

'No. Yes. Not really. Only to see that everything's okay.'

'Romance!' whispered Josie, with shining eyes. 'Can I come?'

'No, of course not!' She looked desperately at her younger sister whose whine was changing to a pout. 'You could help though, you could help a lot.'

Josie thought this over. 'Can I borrow your sleeveless black top with the sequins?'

'Okay.'

'What do you want me to do?'

'Just cover for me tonight. If anyone asks, I'm asleep. And in the morning—' she thought for a minute. 'I'll ring in the morning before they find out I've gone. But if I can't for some reason, tell Mum not to worry. And look—' She fumbled in her bag for her bank statement, and passed it to Josie. It showed her accumulated wages, hardly touched. 'Give that to Dad so he'll see I can pay back the money.'

Josie stared with big eyes. 'You're rich!'

'There wasn't anything to spend it on.'
'How are you getting down?'
'Train. Taxi and train.'
'There won't be any trains, not this late.'
Aptly, the clock struck ten at that moment. Both girls listened, holding their breath, counting the strokes as if they didn't already know what time it was.
'Terry would take you,' said Josie, conscious of doing her less practical sister a favour.
'It's too late to ask him, isn't it?'
'Why? He took Mandy for her baby. He's not busy tonight. I passed the car on my way home.'
'Okay, I'll try.' Hope flamed in Jess's breast. She gave her sister a hug, fastened her bag and opened the door. The poky landing and staircase seemed, for a second, to lead into an abyss, although there were lights down there, and voices in the bar.
'Have you got a skirt I can borrow?' Josie whispered in the background, not wanting to lose any chances.
'There's the red with the plastic belt, you can have that,' she told her, without turning round.
'Sure? Thanks! Good luck!'
Judy, foreshortened, hurried below them with meals on a tray. Jess fled downstairs and whisked out by the back.
It was raining, and there were no taxis about, or much traffic. Terry lived on the hill. His car was still parked in front of his house, and the light was on downstairs. She rang the bell. She could see him inside, watching TV in his jeans and vest. She rang again, for longer, and he got out of his chair and came to the door. Behind him his wife screamed, 'Get your finger off that bell! You'll wake up the kids!'

'What you want to go all that way this tima night?' he said yawning, rubbing his crewcut.

'It's to see a friend.'

'Some friend! What your mama say to me if I take you?'

'It's better than going by train.'

'No trains this tima night.'

'I'll sleep on a bench at the station. She won't like that.'

He looked her over and then he said, 'It'll cost, that distance.'

'I've got money.' She opened her bag so that he could see the wad of notes. He knew she'd been earning. His wife yelled, 'Get that door shut! It's arctic here!'

He reached for his duffle coat and followed her down the path. She got into the back of the car, with one glance at the White Posts in its pool of light at the bottom of the hill. There was no doubt in her mind. She felt calmer than she had for weeks, and presently went to sleep. She slept so well that when they reached Palmers Cross and he roused her for directions, she sat up yawning and rubbing her eyes, astonished because it was still night.

He dropped her at the drive end. There was a light on somewhere in the house; the downstairs windows weren't quite dark.

'Thanks a lot,' she said, as she paid him.

'I'll wait to see you in.'

'It's okay, don't worry.'

'I'll wait.'

The noise of the river was like a welcoming voice. The garden smelt nice in the rain. Her feet crunched on the gravel. She hadn't worked out what she was going to say to Michael when he answered the door, but as she approached she saw that it was standing ajar. She turned and waved to Terry, and as she went in, she heard him drive away. The hall was just the same – furniture, picture, carpets – but the gloss had gone. She guessed that Mrs Drue had stopped coming. She took off her coat and put it automatically on the wooden armchair where callers had always left their coats when Della ruled, and looked round, wondering where the light was coming from. It was more of a pinkish glow upstairs, but there must be someone in the kitchen because the door was brightly underlined. She went down the hall and opened it. The kitchen was glaring hot – a furnace – and as she stared in, horrified, the electric cooker facing the door caught the draught and seemed to burst out at her in a foul smelling explosion. She slammed the door and ran to the hall phone. As she snatched up the mouthpiece, the wires fell away uselessly from the instrument; and at the same time an invisible hand, or draught caught the front door and crashed it shut. But she was thinking of Michael.

She raced upstairs. The acrid smell hurt her nose and made her cough, but she didn't notice any of that. Up here the landing was framed with flame as the skirting boards began to burn. All the doors were open but his; in Della's room, scarlet flowers were creeping up the curtains, her drab magnolia pattern was springing to fiery life. Jess could see at a glance that there was no point in trying to stop this with water. Seeds of fire were germinating everywhere; it looked as though someone had prepared the whole house with inflammable spray, from the way the spurts and frills of flame were spreading. The air was getting hotter; soon the whole place would go up like a tinder box.

She tried Michael's door but it was locked. She thundered on the panels with her fists. She didn't know if he was dead or alive in there, but she banged and shouted. At last she heard footsteps, the key turned, and he looked out, stupefied with sleep. In an instant he came to life. He grasped her wrist and pulled her into his room, turned on the shower and pushed her under it while he scrambled on a shirt and trousers. He drenched himself, and passing her a soaking cloth for her face, muffled his own in a sponge. All this took less than a minute, and they ran out on to the landing. An arrangement of dried flowers went up in front of them with a lick of flame, a scatter of feathery ash. The painted doors had panels and frames of fire. As they fled down the stairs, there was crash from the kitchen, a boiling glare, and the banisters lit simultaneously.

Michael struggled with the front door, but he couldn't get it open. Jess's eyes were huge with terror. The fire was a torturer's net, quickly closing round them. They had only seconds of time. And then she heard somebody laugh.

She spun round, just in time to see the drawing-room door shut. She hurled herself against it with Michael. Together they rushed it, and desperation gave them strength; at the second attempt the bolt gave and they hurtled through. At the same time there was a crash as Christian smashed the window with a chair, and leapt out. They caught a glimpse of him running away between the trees.

The hall was an inferno in the gape that had been the door. Jess pushed back her hair from her scorching face, and climbed out into the garden; Michael followed quickly. Behind them, in the drawing-room, by some curious chance, the picture of Sylvie was the first thing to ignite. The beautiful canvas suddenly blistered, twisting her face into hideous grimaces. It blackened, was consumed; only the frame and stretchers were left on the wall, burning merrily.

Jess lifted up her face to the rain. She was shaking all over. Michael grabbed her hand and they ran, following the river through the garden. When they reached the pool they stopped, gasping for breath. Even here the darkness had a pinky glow, but the destruction in the house was inaudible. The only sound was the rain, dripping steadily among the leaves of the ivy covering the temple. Then Jess felt him squeeze her hand, and she looked where he was looking, at the far side of the pool. Telltale rings were spreading outwards. Someone had surfaced, and was creeping away up the wood.

It was Jess's idea to cross the pool by the balustrade. They sidled along it, hand in hand. The fall was a giddy drop. They faced the other way. Halfway across, they paused, catching sight of the house. It looked like fretwork pierced with scarlet. Every room was blazing.

Jess feared the wood, the rustling leaves underfoot, the whisper of the rain, the closeness of the trees. Michael said quietly, 'He's gone into the tower.' And they went towards it. But Jess had the odd impression that the tower was coming to meet them, rather than the other way round.

When they got close, there was no need to break in. The hinges of the door had worn through long ago, and it had been propped across the entrance. There was some sort of flickering light inside, and an aromatic scent over the predominant smell of leaf mould and damp brick, that she recognized, but couldn't place. Michael kicked in the door and she saw that several torches had been stuck into the earth, the huge scented candles mounted on sticks that were meant to be midge-repellent. They cast a fitful light over the interior of the tower. And presently they saw Christian, halfway up the stone staircase that spiralled all the way to the top. It was strong enough, having been built into the wall. But it wasn't very wide, and there were no handrails left. The tower was perhaps forty feet from top to bottom.

Jess glanced at him, and quickly away. She looked at Michael and saw with a stab of pity that his face was working convulsively. Here on the ground he was powerless, and going up after Christian would solve nothing.

Christian caught sight of them and stopped, spread-eagled against the wall. He called down, with a sort of crazy triumph. His voice echoed as if he was talking into a well.

'You've gone too far this time!' he shouted. 'When people hear the bell they'll come, and then I'll tell them about the cook who was sacked, and came back and set the house on fire!'

'You've got it wrong, Christian,' said Michael. He tried to make his voice calm and strong, although he was trembling. 'Jess is here. She's waiting for you.'

Christian peered down. They stared up at him, hardly daring to breathe.

'No,' he said. 'I don't want her any more.'

'Speak to him,' said Michael in a low voice.

'Christian! Please come down!' She stepped away

from Michael among the torches. He could see her clearly, her face turned up to him, her bright hair.

'But you don't trust me,' he told her, gently. 'I found that out. Never mind. When they hear the bell, they'll come.'

Michael said, 'There's no need to ring the bell. People are coming anyway. The wood's full of people. Come down, you can tell them what you like.'

There was a silence. Then Christian spoke again. 'I don't believe you. It's a trick.' He went on half a dozen steps, using his hands to help him. 'You're too late this time. I'm going to tell them about the perfect husband, and how he held her down when she was swimming, and how she drowned and died.'

Michael was deathly white. Christian went on in a peculiar, sing-song voice. 'It *was* her husband held her down. Just a little time, Michael, a little little time. You'll never know how quick it was. She was mine, and she wanted to die.'

'Oh God,' said Michael under his breath. As he spoke, part of the step below the boy crumbled and fell, weightlessly, until it hit the bottom. It frightened Christian.

'Stop that!' he screamed. 'Leave me alone!'

The bell was barely visible in its metal cradle above his head, but the lever that rocked it was secured to a bracket, which now he reached. He inched upright, and tried to unhook it. Jess could hardly breathe for the thudding of her heart.

The bracket parted, and Christian shouted down at them triumphantly, a meaningless burst of noise that petered out as he tried to shift the rusty bell. Michael gave Jess a shove that sent her stumbling back to the shelter of the doorway, but their eyes were fixed on the gesticulating figure almost at the top of the tower.

'Leave it, you fool!' Michael suddenly yelled, and an instant later, Christian was hurtled to the ground, shrieking, twisting, until he landed face down with his legs doubled up and his arms above his head, like a puppet on a string. And he jerked once, and then he lay still.

Fifteen

The ambulance had come and gone, the fire was out. Michael and Jess were alone in the garden. Behind them, the wreck of the Bell House stood out against the sky, like a stage set for an apocalyptic drama. They were exceedingly dirty, but didn't know it yet, because it was still night, although in the east there was a greyness along the horizon.

For him, the past was burnt out. He might have been just dropped naked into the world.

He said, breaking the silence, 'We'll have to stay together, you realize that.'

'Why?'

Her question was disconcerting.

'I seem to need you, don't you think! That's twice you've come to the rescue.'

'That's no reason for anything.'

'What do you mean?'

'You don't have to be grateful.'

There was a prickly silence. All the time, dawn was coming, It was spreading like water, lightening the sky.

He reached for her hand, and she let him take it.

'You aren't very lady-like in your extremities,' he remarked. 'Look, your hands are almost as big as mine.' He fitted his against hers, and it was true.

'I suppose you'd call me almost old enough to be your father,' he suggested, presently.

'I suppose so, technically.'

'Thanks!' He sounded dashed, and she was surprised, and sorry.

'*Technically*, I said. Doc's a lot older than you are.'

He changed the subject. 'Della will need somewhere to live. The flat in London is big enough for all of us, if you think you could come back.'

Darkness and light were now balanced in the sky, but light was gaining. There was suddenly singing, very small, very high up.

Jess said, 'What's that bird?'

'A lark. – You don't have to decide anything now.' He hesitated. He said, 'Please would you think about it! On a permanent basis.'

'Okay,' she said, quietly. Another lark had risen. The sky quivered with song.

'What's *okay*? Yes, you'll think about it, or yes, you think you'll come? Jess,' he said pitifully, when he had waited for her to reply, and she didn't, 'I'm asking you to marry me.'

And it would happen, as certainly as morning was coming. He put his arms round her and kissed her mouth in a way she couldn't have imagined. Inside she felt she was draining away; except for her heart, and that was like a lark, rising and singing.

Other great reads from ***Red Fox***

Further Red Fox titles that you might enjoy reading are listed on the following pages. They are available in bookshops or they can be ordered directly from us.

If you would like to order books, please send this form and the money due to:

ARROW BOOKS, BOOKSERVICE BY POST, PO BOX 29, DOUGLAS, ISLE OF MAN, BRITISH ISLES. Please enclose a cheque or postal order made out to Arrow Books Ltd for the amount due, plus 22p per book for postage and packing, both for orders within the UK and for overseas orders.

NAME ________________________________

ADDRESS ______________________________

____

Please print clearly.

Whilst every effort is made to keep prices low, it is sometimes necessary to increase cover prices at short notice. If you are ordering books by post, to save delay it is advisable to phone to confirm the correct price. The number to ring is THE SALES DEPARTMENT 071 (if outside London) 973 9700.

Enter the gripping world of the REDWALL saga

REDWALL Brian Jacques

It is the start of the summer of the Late Rose. Redwall Abbey, the peaceful home of a community of mice, slumbers in the warmth of a summer afternoon. The mice are preparing for a great jubilee feast.

But not for long. Cluny is coming! The evil one-eyed rat warlord is advancing with his battle-scarred mob. And Cluny wants Redwall . . .

ISBN 0 09 951200 9 £3.50

MOSSFLOWER Brian Jacques

One late autumn evening, Bella of Brockhall snuggled deep in her armchair and told a story . . .

This is the dramatic tale behind the bestselling *Redwall.* It is the gripping account of how Redwall Abbey was founded through the bravery of the legendary mouse Martin and his epic quest for Salmandastron. Once again, the forces of good and evil are at war in a stunning novel that will captivate readers of all ages.

ISBN 0 09 955400 3 £3.50

MATTIMEO Brian Jacques

Slagar the fox is intent on revenge . . .

On bringing death and destruction to the inhabitants of Redwall Abbey, in particular to the fearless warrior mouse Matthias. Gathering his evil band around him, Slagar plots to strike at the heart of the Abbey. His cunning and cowardly plan is to steal the Redwall children—and Mattimeo, Matthias' son, is to be the biggest prize of all.

ISBN 0 09 967540 4 £3.50

Other great reads from ***Red Fox***

The Maggie Series Joan Lingard

MAGGIE 1: THE CLEARANCE

Sixteen-year-old Maggie McKinley's dreading the prospect of a whole summer with her granny in a remote Scottish glen. But the holiday begins to look more exciting when Maggie meets the Frasers. She soon becomes best friends with James and spends almost all her time with him. Which leads, indirectly, to a terrible accident . . .

ISBN 0 09 947730 0 £1.99

MAGGIE 2: THE RESETTLING

Maggie McKinley's family has been forced to move to a high rise flat and her mother is on the verge of a nervous breakdown. As her family begins to rely more heavily on her, Maggie finds less and less time for her schoolwork and her boyfriend James. The pressures mount and Maggie slowly realizes that she alone must control the direction of her life.

ISBN 0 09 949220 2 £1.99

MAGGIE 3: THE PILGRIMAGE

Maggie is now seventeen. Though a Glaswegian through and through, she is very much looking forward to a cycling holiday with her boyfriend James. But James begins to annoy Maggie and tensions mount. Then they meet two Canadian boys and Maggie finds she is strongly attracted to one of them.

ISBN 0 09 951190 8 £2.50

MAGGIE 4: THE REUNION

At eighteen, Maggie McKinley has been accepted for university and is preparing to face the world. On her first trip abroad, she flies to Canada to a summer au pair job and a reunion with Phil, the Canadian student she met the previous summer. But as usual in Maggie's life, events don't go quite as planned . . .

ISBN 0 09 951260 2 £2.50

Other great reads from **Red Fox**

Haunting fiction for older readers from Red Fox

THE XANADU MANUSCRIPT
John Rowe Townsend

There is nothing unusual about visitors in Cambridge.

So what is it about three tall strangers which fills John with a mixture of curiosity and unease? Not only are they strikingly handsome but, for apparently educated people, they are oddly surprised and excited by normal, everyday events. And, as John pursues them, their mystery only seems to deepen.

Set against a background of an old university town, this powerfully compelling story is both utterly fantastic and oddly convincing.

'An author from whom much is expected and received.' *Economist*

ISBN 0 09 9751801 £2.50

ONLOOKER Roger Davenport

Peter has always enjoyed being in Culver Wood, and dismissed the tales of hauntings, witchcraft and superstitions associated with it. But when he starts having extraordinary visions that are somehow connected with the wood, and which become more real to him than his everyday life, he realizes that something is taking control of his mind in an inexplicable and frightening way.

Through his uneasy relationship with Isobel and her father, a Professor of Archaeology interested in excavating Culver Wood, Peter is led to the discovery of the wood's secret and his own terrifying part in it.

ISBN 0 09 9750708 £2.50

Other great reads from **Red Fox**

Discover the great animal stories of Colin Dann

JUST NUFFIN

The Summer holidays loomed ahead with nothing to look forward to except one dreary week in a caravan with only Mum and Dad for company. Roger was sure he'd be bored.

But then Dad finds Nuffin: an abandoned puppy who's more a bundle of skin and bones than a dog. Roger's holiday is transformed and he and Nuffin are inseparable. But Dad is adamant that Nuffin must find a new home. Is there *any* way Roger can persuade him to change his mind?

ISBN 0 09 966900 5 £1.99

KING OF THE VAGABONDS

'You're very young,' Sammy's mother said, 'so heed my advice. Don't go into Quartermile Field.'

His mother and sister are happily domesticated but Sammy, the tabby cat, feels different. They are content with their lot, never wondering what lies beyond their immediate surroundings. But Sammy is burningly curious and his life seems full of mysteries. Who is his father? Where has he gone? And what is the mystery of Quartermile Field?

ISBN 0 09 957190 0 £2.50